POWERS

POWERS

DEBORAH LYNN JACOBS

A Deborah Brodie Book

ROARING BROOK PRESS

New Milford, Connecticut

A Deborah Brodie Book
Published by Roaring Brook Press
Roaring Brook Press is a division of Holtzbrinck Publishing Holdings
Limited Partnership
143 West Street, New Milford, Connecticut 06776

Library of Congress Cataloging-in-Publication Data

Jacobs, Deborah Lynn.
Powers / by Deborah Lynn Jacobs.
p. cm.
"A Deborah Brodie Book."
Summary: Gwen and Adrian, two teens with psychic powers, use
their abilities to get what they want and need from each other.
ISBN-13: 978-1-59643-112-6
ISBN-10: 1-59643-112-1
[1. Psychic ability—Fiction. 2. Visions—Fiction.] I. Title.

PZ7.J15213Po 2006
[Fic]—dc22

2005028750

10 9 8 7 6 5 4 3 2 1

Roaring Brook Press books are available for special promotions and
premiums. For details, contact: Director of Special Markets,
Holtzbrinck Publishers.

Book design by Angela Carlino
Printed in the United States of America
First edition September 2006

*To Keith, who has been teaching me about
computers since he was eight and I was . . .
uh . . . old enough to be his mother.*

Acknowledgments

I'd like to thank my husband, David, for supporting me emotionally and financially as I went through the multiple rewrites of this book.

Thank you, Steven Chudney, my awesome agent, for believing in me.

Thank you, Deborah Brodie, my gentle editor, who made this whole process positive, affirming, and *fun!*

To my son and daughter, Keith and Kathryn—I can't thank you enough for all the times you read my rough drafts, made suggestions, and helped me weed out the dialogue that didn't ring true.

Thanks also to my (then) teen readers: Ashley Stocks, Erica Niemiec, J. Garnet Woodburn, and Lauren Jia, who were most gracious with their time and advice.

This novel went through many revisions, helped immensely by my critique partners in: Writers with Wings, the Newberries, Writers' Ink, and OPUS.

A special thanks to Candace J. Tremps for taking me under her Wings.

MONDAY, JANUARY 6

Gwen

Every night, for seven nights, I dreamed of him. Every morning, for seven mornings, I awoke drenched in cold, slippery sweat, whispering to myself: just a dream.

But was it? It felt *real*, more like I'd *lived* it than dreamed it. The staccato rhythm of his boots, echoing down the corridor. His black leather trench coat, swooping behind him like a cape. The way he stood in the doorway of my English class—eyes hidden behind mirrored sunglasses, his posture perfect, physically commanding.

In other words, he was an arrogant jerk. A fake. Outwardly confident; inwardly afraid. A dangerous combination; someone you can't trust.

How did I know? I'm a Watcher, an observer of human behavior. Eighty percent of all communication is nonverbal. It's what you *don't* say that says the most—a shifting of the eyes, a gesture, a subtle intake of breath. As a Watcher, I can sum a person up in less than ten seconds. And I am never wrong.

The dream repeated each night, alternating with nightmarish images.

Night one: the stranger.

Night two: a house consumed by flames, lighting up the night sky.

Night three: a white skull, floating in inky blackness.

Night four: a child-sized casket, its lid up and waiting.

Night five, six, seven: a kaleidoscope—the stranger, the skull, a house on fire, a casket, all tied together.

I tell myself there is no reason to fear this person. His kind and my kind don't mix. He won't notice me. I'm wallpaper. On a bad day, linoleum.

But each morning I awaken, drenched in cold, slippery sweat.

Adrian

First impressions last two years.

That's what Mrs. Ghee drummed into us, two years ago, back in ninth grade. Make a good first impression. Firm handshake. Good eye contact. Look confident, as if you can do the job. People believe what they see. Remember that.

I stare at the door of my new school. My fingers itch for a smoke. The sudden, intense craving takes me by surprise. I gave up smoking a year ago. Didn't enjoy being a slave to my addiction. I like to be in control.

I go inside, wander the halls, searching for my locker. People flow past me. I'm lost, but I march along as if I know where I'm heading.

My gut twists in a killer of a cramp. *Not again.* I dry-swallow an antidiarrhea pill. It slips sideways, sticks like a piece of chalk in my throat. I gag. I sound like Cleo, my cat, coughing up a fur ball.

"Need help?" asks a girl. She's tall, nearly my height, red hair, green eyes.

"Bubbler," I gasp.

She giggles. "What?"

"Water."

"Water fountain?" She leads me to a bubbler, not ten feet away. I gulp water and wash down the pill. "Thanks."

She smiles. She's wearing a short top and low jeans. In between is a smooth stretch of tanned skin. She wears a green jewel in her belly button. The same color as her eyes.

"I'm Melissa," she says.

"Adrian Black." I stick out my hand as if this is a job interview. Smooth move. But she doesn't seem to notice. She slips her hand into mine, shakes it as though we were doing something completely normal.

She giggles again. "See you around."

"See ya." I keep my voice steady, hiding another gut spasm. I need a restroom, fast. And another pill.

By the time I find a restroom and take care of things, the bell rings. No time to find my locker or get rid of my coat.

I walk into my first class: English. Okay. Deep breath, shoulders back. Make it good. People believe what they see.

Gwen

Monday, January 6. I wrote the date in a fresh notebook. English 11. Second semester. Miss Bliss.

I rubbed my eyes and stared at the door of the classroom. I told myself Miss Bliss would be the next person through that door. She'd start the lesson and I would relax. The stranger wasn't coming.

Then I heard it. The decisive rhythm of footsteps in the corridor. I strained my ears to detect the faint *swoosh* of a full-length leather coat. Then, he appeared in the doorway, exactly as I had dreamed him: black hair, high cheekbones, strong jaw, sensual lips.

The stranger pushed aside his coat, shoved his hands into his pockets in a seemingly casual gesture. But I knew there was nothing casual about it. He was drawing attention to himself, to his broad shoulders, narrow waist, lean torso.

People noticed. Most of the girls; some of the guys.

From the tiny movements of his head, I could tell he was surveying the room from behind the cover of his sunglasses. Putting us into two categories: worth his notice, and not worth his notice.

His survey slid past me. *Good.*

The stranger dropped into the desk behind Melissa. Big surprise, there, eh? He stuck one long leg out into the aisle, claiming his territory. He leaned toward Melissa, claiming her.

"We meet again," he said in a radio announcer's voice, practically dripping testosterone. Did he work at that? Practice to get the timbre just right?

Melissa flawlessly performed the first step of the human mating ritual. She tilted her chin down, then glanced up through her eyelashes. He responded by flicking off his sunglasses, hanging them on the front of his T-shirt, and leaning closer.

Melissa moved to step two, the invitation to touch, by running her hand down the length of her arm. The stranger didn't hesitate. He reached out, briefly touched her hand with his own, then drew it back.

Unreal.

"We meet again," Melissa said.

How original. I tried to stifle my laughter, but I let out a small sound despite my efforts.

Snake-quick, the stranger whipped his head around. *Good one, Gwen. Break the cardinal rule. Let him know you're Watching.*

His eyes shone an unearthly blue, somewhere between topaz and turquoise. I'd seen that color only once before, when my parents took me to a glacier in the Rockies. The meltwater had run down the cracks in the ice, subzero, clear blue, and totally devoid of life.

Adrian

There's one in every school. Some person who isn't buying it. She gives me this *look*, like I've somehow broken some rule. She hates Melissa, you can tell. Don't get me wrong. I've no illusions about Melissa. She's probably been with a dozen guys. That doesn't bother me. At least she's honest. Offers the goods right up front.

But this other girl, totally different story. Long brown hair, parted in the middle so it half-hides her face. Big, thick glasses. Sloppy gray sweatshirt, which either hides a fat body or a gorgeous body.

A fat body, I'm guessing. Hates the pretty girls, like Melissa, because she has never felt pretty. Hates me already, for some unknown reason. But, that *look* she gave me. As if she's almost afraid of me. Well, yeah, makes sense. Fat girls are always afraid of hot guys. That whole rejection scenario.

It bugs me, though. Her judging me. Like she has the right, living out here in the middle of nowhere, to judge anyone.

Of all the moves we've made, this is the worst. Rocky Waters, Ontario, Canada. Ten thousand people hunkered down in the middle of virgin forest and ice-locked lakes. One road in. One road out. Dad calls it God's Country. Sure, I get it. No one else wanted it.

The teacher, what's her name, Blissful or something, is droning on about our syllabus. My mind drifts back to this morning. I'd checked before breakfast to make sure my car, a vintage '69 Mustang, would start. It didn't.

"Mom, where's the charger?" I yelled, stomping back into the house.

"Basement," she called, from the kitchen.

"Basement," I mumbled. "Not the garage. Figures."

While the battery charged, I whipped up my usual breakfast—a yogurt, fruit, and protein-powder shake. Mom was wiping down the cupboards. She does that every time we move. You can't tell by appearances, she says. Yeah, who knows what lurks in those cupboards. Cholera, dysentery, bubonic plague. Could be anything.

I poured my shake into a glass and set the blender down. Hard. It tipped over, spilling the last of my shake onto the counter. Swearing, I wiped it up.

"Why here," I snapped, suddenly furious with every-thing—the move, Dad, Mom.

"I'm sorry?" Mom asked, poking her head out of the cupboard.

"Why here?" I repeated. "Why did you agree to move? Why couldn't you back me up for once?"

Mom stripped off her rubber gloves, spoke as if she'd memorized the speech. "Your father has always wanted his own privately owned, family-operated business, Adrian—"

"Why *here*?" I interrupted.

She hesitated. "Your father felt compelled to move here. It was as if this place called to him."

"What do you mean? Called to him?"

"He said it was for you. He said you belonged here."

"That's a load of—" I clamped my jaw shut. I have more control than to swear at my mother.

Mom came over, and put one hand on my face. It smelled like bleach. "It's going to work out, Adrian. It always does."

It never does, I thought, going back out to the garage. Moving every few years wasn't the great adventure Mom made it out to be. Just when you start making friends, you move. You re-create yourself, over and over. After a while, you forget who you are. You make it up as you go. As long as it works, as long as it gets you what you want, that's all that matters.

Gwen

"So, this new guy. Adrian Black. Is he *the one?*" Joanne asked, plunking down her plate of poutine. The combination of French fries layered with gravy and cheese curds looked like a dog's dinner, but smelled fantastic.

"The one *what?*" I jabbed my fork into my so-called lunch, a salad with fat-free dressing. Why had my cousin inherited all the skinny genes? No justice, eh?

Joanne struggled to speak around her mouthful of fries. "*Him.* The man of your dreams."

I stole one of her fries, slid it through half-congealed gravy, and devoured it before answering.

"The boy *in* my dreams," I clarified.

"What does he look like?" Joanne finger-combed her sandy-blonde hair. It fell in layered waves, framing her delicate face and light brown eyes.

I shoved aside my own crap-brown hair and pushed my glasses up on my nose. "Ugly. Big yellow teeth. Acne. *Bad* acne."

Joanne went into a coughing spasm. I leaned back as a shower of milkshake flew my way. "Not what I heard," she said, once she stopped hacking.

"Well, you heard wrong."

"What are you so afraid of?" Joanne asked.

"Him. I saw *him*. I saw houses on fire. Coffins. Skulls. It's all connected. Ergo, he's dangerous."

Joanne sighed. "Honestly, Gwen, you are the only person on the planet who uses the word 'ergo.' In my opinion, you never got over Stone."

That stung. Oh, did it sting. Stone. Grade eight. Back then, I was fat, not merely heavy, like now. Add to that braces and glasses. So I should have been suspicious when Stone, the cutest guy in the school, asked me to our grade eight graduation dance. "My parents and I will pick you up at six." He didn't show. You know what they say: if it seems too good to be true . . .

Later, Melissa told me that Joanne paid Stone twenty bucks to take me to the dance. He grabbed the money and ran. That hurt, to think my own cousin figured I was so pathetic that she had to buy me a date. My pride prevented me from confronting her.

"Joanne, I got over Stone a long time ago," I told her. "Drop it, okay?"

Joanne wasn't listening. I turned around, following her rapt gaze, to see Adrian swaggering through the cafeteria. He was coatless now, his muscles bulging under butt-tight jeans and a black T-shirt. He looked like a movie star in a sea of extras.

"Oh, wow," Joanne said. "I've got to meet him."

"You have a boyfriend. Conrad, remember?"

"I'm thinking of breaking it off." She glanced two tables over to where Conrad ate lunch with his hockey friends. "He's too possessive. And, he never opens up. I want a guy who can be real with me."

"He's already latched onto Melissa," I said, now desperate.

"What?"

"English class. Had his hands all over her."

Joanne looked over to the table beside us. Sure enough, Melissa was standing up, her eyes on Adrian.

"She's moving in," Joanne said. "*Let me go!*" She pulled free of my grasp and dashed to the front of the cafeteria. Adrian turned around, balancing a loaded tray, searching for a place to sit.

Melissa was fast, but Joanne was faster. From this distance, I couldn't hear what she said to Adrian, but it must have worked. He followed her back to our table. Melissa veered off, acting as if she hadn't been aiming for him after all.

Run. Run and hide.

"Adrian, this is my cousin, Gwen," said Joanne, sitting down beside me.

"Yeah, Gwen's in my first class." Adrian sent me a smile. A pity smile, to make the fat girl's day. What did he expect me to do? Swoon?

"So, Adrian, where are you living?" prompted Joanne.

"Eagle Lake Road."

"You guys bought the Anderson place?" Joanne asked. "Hey, Gwen, you used to babysit for the Andersons, remember?"

I nodded.

"Wow," Joanna continued, "we're almost neighbors. Go another two klicks and you get to my place."

"Klicks?"

"Kilometers. Gwen and I are cousins. Did I mention that? Gwen and her mom live like five houses from me."

Adrian raised an eyebrow.

"Gwen's dad is gone," Joanne explained. "Died like, what, three years ago, Gwen?"

"Yes." Three years and four months ago. Heart attack. The day before my fourteenth birthday.

"I'm sorry," Adrian said, but it sounded like the automatic "I'm sorry" that people always say.

I shrugged, as if it were no big deal.

"So, Adrian," continued Joanne, "tell us all about yourself."

"What do you want to know?" He spoke so quietly you had to strain to hear. Nice control tactic.

"Where are you from?"

"Milwaukee. Before that, Philadelphia, Chicago, other places."

Milwaukee came out as Ma-wakee. His accent was a mix of eastern seaboard twang and midwestern drawl.

"Why'd you move around?" Joanne continued.

"My dad's work."

"What's he do?" Joanne was a bulldog. Once she caught hold of a person, she didn't let go. Adrian's ears turned transparently pink.

"He bought the funeral home in town," he said.

"Oh, so that explains Gwen's dr—"

I kicked her under the table.

"Her what?" asked Adrian.

"Uh, nothing," Joanne said, throwing me a dirty look. "So, your dad runs the business?"

"Yeah," Adrian said, his accent turning it into two syllables. "I help out—shoveling snow, cleaning, greeting visitors, maintaining the vehicles. Dad does everything else. The arrangements. The embalming."

"Gross," said Joanne, then clapped her hand over her mouth. That's Joanne for you: speak first, think later.

Adrian leaned toward her. "Jo, I'll let you in on a little secret. The embalming? No big deal. Once they're gone, they're gone. They don't complain." He leaned back, folded his arms. "It's the relatives who can be a real pain."

"Very sympathetic, for an undertaker's son," I couldn't help but say.

"It's a business," Adrian said. "At the end of the day, my dad goes home like anyone else. No need to get emotionally involved."

Wow, he was *cold*.

He shot a sharp look at me, as if he knew what I was thinking, then turned his attention to his lunch. He'd bought two grilled chicken sandwiches. He removed the chicken from the rolls and set the rolls aside. He scraped the mayonnaise off the chicken, and cut it up into bite-sized pieces. He piled it on top of his salad, then ate precisely, chewing slowly and washing down each bite with part-skim milk.

"Fry?" Joanne offered him. A faint look of disgust crossed his face as he looked at her poutine, but he quickly hid it.

"No, thanks."

Joanne stuffed in another mouthful, then mumbled around her food. "So, you like it here?"

Adrian held up a finger, indicating he was still chewing. Then he leaned forward. I knew his next words would be something slimy like, "I like *you* very much, Jo."

Maybe he caught my expression. He stopped, pulled his hand back. "It's cold," he said. "My car wouldn't start at first."

"Didja plug 'er in?" Joanne said, chewing.

"Sorry?"

Joanne swallowed. "Did you plug in your block heater?"

"Uh, no," he admitted.

Ha! He had no idea what a block heater was. Even Joanne caught it. "You don't know what that is, do you?" she asked.

"Sure, I do," he said, not very convincingly.

"It's a heater that warms your engine block," said Joanne. "You plug your car in overnight. You'll need it if the temperature goes down to thirty."

"Thirty? That's barely freezing," he said.

"Thirty *below*, Centigrade," Joanne said. "In Fahrenheit, that's like, uh, what is it, Gwen?"

"Twenty or twenty-five below, Fahrenheit," I estimated. "Forty below is the same on both scales."

Adrian deigned to look at me. He raised one eyebrow and tilted his head.

"Trust her," Joanne said. "Gwen's a genius."

Thanks, Joanne. Fat and a genius. I wonder why the guys don't flock to me.

Adrian turned his attention back to Joanne. "So, where can I get a block heater, Jo?"

"Canadian Tire," she said. "Hey, how's about I meet you after school. If your car doesn't start, I can give you a lift."

"Okay." He was all smiles now.

"No," I said.

"Why not?" said Joanne.

"We have that thing after school."

"What thing?"

I kicked her. "*That* thing."

"Oh. *That* thing." She gave me a look that said we'd have to talk about this later. "Uh, sorry, Adrian. Another time?"

"Sure." Big smile, showing perfect white teeth. I bet he bleached them.

Joanne checked her watch. "Oops. Forgot. I have a meeting before the next class."

"Let me guess," Adrian said, still smiling. "Cheerleader?"

"Debate Team," Joanne said, with a perceptible edge to her voice.

Adrian's head jerked back, a bare millimeter, but enough for a Watcher to notice. "See you later, Jo," he said, recovering.

No way. Not while I was around. What a predator. He was *not* getting my cousin.

Once Joanne was gone, I said, "Her name's Joanne, by the way. Not Jo."

"I'll try to remember that," he replied, eyes narrowed. Then he turned his attention to his food. I had been dismissed.

Jerk, I thought, getting up to leave.

I looked back to see a half-puzzled, half-angry expression in his big baby blues. It was almost as if I'd spoken out loud. But I hadn't. Had I?

Adrian

What's with her, anyway? Telling me in that stuck-up voice, "Her name is Joanne, not Jo." Then she calls me a jerk. If this is Canadian hospitality, I can do without it.

I finish eating, then go out to the parking lot to run my car for a while to keep the engine from freezing. While it's warming up, I call home.

"Hello," answers a male voice. Great. My father.

"Is Mom there?"

"She's busy." I hear Mom in the background, rattling dishes.

"Tell Mom I'll be home late. I'm going to Canadian Tire to get a block heater."

"Good idea," says Dad. "I'll reimburse you."

"Fair enough," I say. "Since you're the reason I need one."

That meets with hard silence. Dad's not one for pissing matches. He lets the silence sink in, then says, "I'll let your mother know you'll be late."

His voice is as subzero as the wind that whips off the lake, freezing my fingers before I reach the warmth of the school.

Gwen

Had I called him a jerk out loud? That wasn't like me. Maybe I'd muttered it under my breath. He made me so furious. The way he moved in on Joanne, repeating her name like some smarmy used car salesman, calling her "Jo" like they'd been friends for years.

And Joanne, so naive, falling for him. Someone has to watch out for her. She has no sense where boys are concerned. Look at Conrad. All romantic gestures, flowers and chocolate and love notes. And Joanne fell for it. Meanwhile, she even looks at another guy and Conrad goes ballistic. Something wrong there.

I drove slowly through town, heading for my work placement as a student photographer at *Rocky Waters Press*. It was a gorgeous day. Twenty-five below, deep blue sky, no wind. I reached the newspaper office and entered through the back door, leading to the presses. I loved the roar and rumble, the rush of papers speeding along the rolls, the inky smell of the fresh newsprint. I grabbed a paper, and checked out the photo on the front page.

A house on fire, with flames reaching into the night. *Please no. Don't let this be happening.*

The cutline said: "House Destroyed By Early Morning Fire." There was little else, except to say the Rocky Waters Volunteer Fire Department had responded quickly but was unable to put out the blaze.

I stopped by Doug, my editor's, office. "You busy?" I asked.

"Hey, kiddo, grab a seat," replied Doug, motioning with one ape-hairy arm at the chair in front of his battered oak desk.

"Any more on this?" I asked, pointing to the photograph.

"Police gave more details about an hour ago," Doug said. "Sad story. Seven-year-old boy died. Parents out of town. Older sister supposed to be babysitting, but she was at her boyfriend's place."

A small casket, its lid up and waiting.

"You okay, kiddo?" Doug asked. "You look as if you've seen a ghost."

"Um, fine," I managed to say. "Uh, did the kid set the fire?"

"Not unless he was playing with gasoline and a pile of rags in the basement," Doug said.

"Arson?"

"*Suspected* arson," he clarified. "Look, I'd like you to get a shot of the wreckage. We'll run it tomorrow with the latest from the police."

He handed over my assignment sheet—take a photo of the burned-out house, get a few shots of the penny drive at the elementary school, and a photo of the monthly birthday party at the seniors' center. Okay. I could do that. Take the shots, get the names, triple-check the spelling, turn in my photos and cutlines.

"Oh, and Gwen? If the police are poking around the fire scene, try to get a statement, okay?"

"Oh, no. I'm a photographer, not a reporter."

"C'mon, kiddo," said Doug. "We've been through this before. Hard to make a living strictly as a photographer. You need to spread your wings."

No way. Watchers watch. They take pictures from behind the safety of the camera lens.

Doug gave me directions to the house. Great. A country road. Narrow, treacherously icy, winding between rock cliffs and swamps. Not to mention the deer that leap across the road when you least expect them. Let's hope I don't crack up Mom's old Volvo.

After twenty minutes of white-knuckle driving, I crested a hill and there it was. *The house I'd watched burn.*

At least the police weren't there. Small comfort.

A vile stench hit me as I got out of the car, a combination of charred wood and scorched insulation. Only one corner of the house remained standing. I moved closer, holding my breath. There it was, hanging on the wall. *A poster of a skull, bone-white on a black background.*

I wanted to jump back in the car and drive, get away, *run.* I reminded myself I had a job to do. I snapped off a dozen photos, catching the house from all angles. But I knew the shot Doug would choose.

The skull, floating in blackness, framed by charred wood.

Adrian

Cold enough to freeze your balls. I'd always thought that was just an expression. Not at twenty-five below, it isn't.

I drive to Canadian Tire after school. My block heater will take an hour to install, so I decide to check out the town. Bad move. My sinus cavities fill with ice. My nose hairs are as brittle as glass. If I sneeze, they'll shatter. And my toes? I'll probably have to amputate.

I pass a store called Freshly Ground. I go inside, order a triple espresso and gulp it down steaming hot. As I pay for the coffee, something happens. I feel shivery hot and sweaty cold, like an ice cube tossed on a sizzling grill. Beside the cash register, along with the candy bars and breath mints, is a collection of key chains. My hand closes on one.

"How much?" I ask.

"A toonie," the woman responds.

"A what?"

"Two dollar coin. You new around here?"

"Yes."

"Thought so. Your accent, eh?"

I'm thinking, I don't have an accent. *She does.* But I say nothing as I hand her a two-dollar coin. It's large and heavy, with a copper disc inside a nickel ring.

"Here you go then. Have yourself a good one," she says.

I'm outside before I take a closer look at my purchase. A cheap plastic skull, about two inches long, is attached to the metal key ring. The skull's moveable jaw drops down in an obscene grin. Its black eye sockets stare at me.

I must be crazy. I toss the skull into a trash can and walk on.

After half a block, I turn back. I stare into the trash. The skull grins up at me. *Take me home,* it says.

"No way." I walk away. And stop. Without understanding why, I pick the skull out of the trash. Half a dozen times in the next five blocks, I take it out and throw it away.

But each time, it calls me back.

TUESDAY, JANUARY 7

Gwen

Every Tuesday and Thursday, Joanne and I had opposite lunches. On these days, I ate alone, doing what I did best: Watching.

I propped up my current novel, *Pride and Prejudice*, and dug into my spinach salad. Melissa and her entourage swept past and sat at the table next to me. A moment later, Adrian sauntered in, dressed in jeans and a light blue shirt, worn open over a dark T-shirt.

Yeah, heads turned.

Adrian favored me with a glance, but didn't go so far as to nod or say hello. His left eyebrow rose in surprise when he saw the title of my book. As if I cared.

"May I join you?" he asked Melissa, turning his back on me.

Of course you can join her, I thought. Anyone, anywhere, anytime. That's our Melissa.

Melissa nearly fell off her chair moving over for him. Her friends shifted one down to accommodate Adrian. They reminded me of a gaggle of geese, all honking quietly. Melissa, the head goose, glared at them to shut up.

"So," Melissa said.

"So," Adrian replied. He tapped his fingers on the table. Nerves? Interesting.

Abruptly, he stopped tapping, leaned toward Melissa and spoke in his sexy just-for-you voice. "Want to know a secret? I can read your mind."

Spare me.

"Read my mind?" Melissa actually batted her eyelashes at him.

"Sure. I'm psychic. I channel the basic life force of the universe," he said.

I nearly choked. *Basic life force?*

"Give me your hand," he crooned.

Melissa complied. Adrian closed his eyes as if in deep concentration. "You've broken up with your boyfriend."

"That's right. How did you know?" she gushed.

Well, babe, might be the white spot on your hand

where you took off the ring. Melissa had been dating Stone since grade eight, in an on-again, off-again relationship. Right now it was off. Melissa is high-maintenance.

"He didn't give you the love and attention you deserve," Adrian continued.

I inhaled a piece of spinach and coughed furiously to dislodge it. Adrian watched me, head tilted, eyebrow lifted.

"Are you all right?" he asked.

"Fine, thank you," I replied with as much dignity as I could muster. I wasn't finished eating, but I'd seen enough.

Like seeks like. He was welcome to her.

Adrian

"Like seeks like?" I turn around, but she's gone.

"Huh?" Melissa says.

"Is that a Canadian expression?" I ask.

"Is what?"

"Like seeks like."

"I didn't say that," Melissa said with a frown.

"No. Gwen did."

Melissa gives me a blank stare. The other girls look at me as if I'm crazy. Whoa. Think fast.

"Guess I read her mind," I joke.

They stare at me with mouths gaped open. They look like a bunch of birds, like geese or something.

I almost expect them to honk.

WEDNESDAY, JANUARY 8

Gwen

I'd had the strangest dream. A herd of deer crossed Bjorn Bay to reach the first island. Stalking them was a gray wolf. Symbolic. The deer are obviously Melissa and her group. And guess who is the wolf?

Only it didn't feel symbolic. It felt *real*. Like the dream of Adrian, the house fire, the skull, the dead child. *What's happening to me?*

I showered, pulled on a pair of jeans and a sweatshirt,

and joined Mom in the car. She drove cautiously, creeping around corners and putt-putting along the icy sections.

"We're here," she said, arriving at the bakery where she'd worked since high school. She got out and I slid into the driver's seat. "Be careful," she said.

"I'll be careful," I promised. It was our morning ritual. Be careful of what, I wasn't sure, but when I said the words some of the tightness eased in her face.

I waited for the last minute to go to English class, dreading the fact that Adrian would be there. I needn't have worried. He ignored me when I walked into the room.

Arrogant jerk.

At lunchtime, I was relieved to find Joanne alone at our table.

"You sure you can eat all that?" Joanne asked by way of greeting. She pointed to my Caesar salad without dressing and my bottled water.

"We can't all eat like you, Joanne."

"Who peed in your cereal this morning?"

"I didn't have cereal this morning. Nothing else, either."

Joanne made an exasperated huffing noise. "How often do I have to say it? Read my lips. *You are not fat.*"

"Read *my* lips," I replied. "You're my cousin. It's your job to say that."

Joanne stewed for a minute, had a few bites of her chicken strips with barbeque sauce, then changed the subject. "So, I broke up with Conrad."

I glanced over at Conrad. He sat with the boys, his beetle-brown eyes trained on Joanne. He held his fork in a fist-like grip, mounding the macaroni and cheese on his plate and then mashing it down.

"Looks as if he took it pretty hard," I said.

"Too bad. He told me he didn't want me talking to Adrian. So I told him it's over." Joanne brushed her hands together in a dismissive gesture.

In the next second, she caught sight of Adrian.

"Hey, Adrian! Over here." I kicked her under the table. She kicked me back. "What is *wrong* with you?" she hissed.

I opened my mouth to answer, but Adrian arrived. He carried a lunch tray with tuna salad, yogurt, and an apple.

"Hi, Jo," he said, with his ultrabright smile.

At the next table, Conrad stabbed his macaroni.

"So, how's our amazing mind reader?" Joanne asked.

Adrian pulled the lid off his yogurt. A tiny bit splashed on his long-sleeved black shirt. He dabbed at it, frowned, and smiled at her. "I'm great. How are you, Jo?"

Right then, if I could have shot a lightning bolt at him, I would have.

"Joanne," I said, "he can't read minds."

"Sure he can," said Joanne. "I heard he read Melissa's mind yesterday."

I groaned. "Parlor tricks, Joanne. He makes general suggestions to people, watches their reactions, then plays on them. He's a fake."

"I'm sitting right here, Gwen." Adrian's voice held an undercurrent of anger.

"Fine. *You're* a fake," I said to his face.

"Whoa, easy, boys and girls, no bickering," Joanne said. "Let's put it to the test. Here, Adrian, tell me what I'm thinking."

Adrian reached across the table toward Joanne. His shirt pulled back, revealing strong wrists, long fingers, and meticulously clean nails. He closed his eyes as if in deep concentration. "You are thinking you'd like to go to a movie with me tonight."

"No," said Joanne. "I mean yes."

"Which is it?"

"No, I was thinking about my History quiz. But, yes. I'd love to go to a movie with you."

"No," I said, too loud, too fast.

"Why not?"

"Joanne has a boyfriend, right, Joanne?"

"But, I—"

I kicked her again.

"Joanne already has a boyfriend," I said to Adrian. I said each word slowly and clearly, so there would be no mistake.

"A-a-l-l-l r-i-i-ight." He drew the words out, mimicking me. Mocking me. I wanted to kick him, too, only *hard*.

Then he gave Joanne his big, fake smile. "I can wait my turn."

Yeah, in a pig's patootie, I thought.

Adrian's head whipped around. For a second, I thought he'd heard me. His eyes held me, immobilized me, like an animal in a leg-hold trap.

"You're afraid of me." He made it a statement. A challenge.

"No." But my pulse raced.

"Give me your hand. If it's a trick, you have nothing to fear," said Adrian.

"Don't patronize me!" It's hard to say "patronize" when you are gritting your teeth, but I managed.

"I'm not patronizing you."

It was his voice that made up my mind for me. He'd dropped it down, slow and even and hypnotic. He thought he could control me with that voice. No way.

I let him take my hand. The cold blue flame in his eyes held me, seared me.

"Do you feel it?" he asked.

"No."

"It's a warm tingle, isn't it? In your hands, moving up your arms, like a current."

"No." My hands tingled with warmth. It moved up my arms like a current.

"Don't lie to me, Gwen."

"Let me go."

"No." Then he noticed my scar, a raised white ridge between my index and second finger. He ran his thumb lightly over the scar tissue.

I flinched. I hated that scar. I'd earned it through sheer stupidity, trying to separate frozen burgers with a steak knife.

"It's never going to go away," Adrian said in a condescending voice. "I still can't believe you did that."

My heart thumped unevenly. "What do you mean?"

"Used Crazy Glue to seal the cut."

I swallowed. "How did you know that?"

"Who could forget?" Adrian said, shaking his head. "All that blood, and you insisting you didn't need stitches."

I looked at Joanne. She looked at me. "Uh, Adrian?" she said. "You just got here. You couldn't possibly know that."

Adrian dropped my hand. His voice wavered, as if he was unsure of what had happened. "But, I saw it, Jo. I felt it. The knife, so sharp, it didn't hurt. Not at first. Not until the blood spurted out. Over my shirt, my white shirt."

He stopped, stared at me.

"No, not my shirt. Your blouse. You never got the stain out, did you, Gwen?"

"Wow." Joanne jiggled in her chair with excitement. "Wow, this proves it!"

I froze. "You told him, Joanne, right? You're both in on the trick."

"Nobody told me, Gwen. It was as if the memory was in my own head. I can still feel it. . . . " Adrian's voice trailed off as he rubbed the webbing between the first and second fingers of his own hand.

My chair clattered to the floor as I pushed away. Heads turned toward me, but I didn't care. I ran.

Adrian

She takes off, not bothering to get her coat. I follow her to the parking lot. The frigid air slices through me.

"Gwen, wait," I call.

She backs up against an old maroon Volvo wagon. "Go away."

I feel a wave of fear, so strong I could reach out and gather it in my hands. And I realize it's not *my* fear.

It's hers.

"How are you doing it?" she demands.

"I'm not doing anything."

"You expect me to believe that?"

"I don't believe it myself. It's as if I'm reading your mind. Did you send me the thoughts? Is that it? Are you telepathic?" I'm babbling like an idiot.

I'm not sending you thoughts. I can't read your mind.

"Are you sure? Have you ever tried?"

"Tried what?"

"Tried to read minds?"

"I didn't say that."

"Sure you did. I heard you."

I didn't say that.

This time I watch her lips. They aren't moving. My head buzzes. I'm hearing her thoughts. I'm so charged I could light up a city.

"Think something else to me," I say.

"No. Leave me alone." She fumbles to get her key into the door lock, but her hand is shaking too much.

"Look, you're too upset to drive." I reach around to take the keys from her hand. Our bodies touch. I feel a surge of energy, strong and startling, move between us.

She yelps, and jabs her elbow, catching me in the stomach.

"*Ow*. What was that for?"

"Don't touch me. Don't ever touch me again, or I'll—"

"What is *wrong* with you?"

Her hands are on her hips. She's not afraid now. She's angry. I feel it like I felt the fear. And another emotion. Loathing.

Loathing? *For me?*

"You don't even know me," I say.

"I know your kind." *Like Stone.* "Stay away from us!"

"Us?"

"Me. And Joanne."

Jo? No way.

"No one tells me what to do," I say.

"I just did," she spits out.

I'm *this* close to losing it. I watch her get into her car, slam the door, rev the engine. I still sense her energy, crackling in the air. The feeling fades as she drives away.

Gwen

My hands shook on the wheel as I drove. How dare he?

Nobody tells me what to do.

It was like a summer storm rolling in across the lake.

The air shifts, turns cold. Thunder rolls. Lightning flashes. The water stirs.

The storm envelops you in its fury. You run inside, seeking shelter. Rain slashes, battering the windows, trying to get in.

For now, you are safe. But safety is an illusion. Between you and the storm, there is nothing but a thin sheet of glass.

Adrian

What just happened? When I touched her hand, I'd felt a power, an energy, like a house current, coursing just under her skin. It was like drinking in sunlight, intoxicating, addictive. One hit, and I'm hooked. I want more. I *need* more. Only one problem. She wants nothing to do with me.

So, I'm going to need an ally. Jo. I ask someone where to find her locker and go there after school.

I'm just in time. She's putting on her jacket, getting ready to leave. She runs her hands under her hair, flipping it over the collar. I move into her personal space, tuck a wisp of hair behind her ear. She makes a quiet sound, like, "hmmm," and leans toward me.

Easy Adrian. Stay on target. I jam my hands resolutely into my pockets.

"No *thing* after school today?" I tease.

"Uh, well, we uh . . ." Her eyes are light brown, almost the color of beach sand. I feel warm for the first time in days.

I let her off the hook. "Want a ride home?"

"Yeah, thanks," Jo says. "My mom drives me in, in the morning, but I get stuck taking the bus home and that's a fifty-minute ride, even though it's only half an hour by car, but that's because we go down all those stupid roads to drop people off, eh?"

She says the whole thing in one breath, I swear, pronouncing "mom" like "mum." Coming from her, it's cute. The snow squeaks under our boots as we walk to my car.

"Nice car," Jo says, running a hand over my red metallic paint job.

"Thanks," I say, opening her door. She slides in and smiles.

Forget Gwen. Then I remember that rush of energy. Better still, why not have it both ways?

My tires scrunch on the frozen snow as I pull out of the parking lot. "So, about that movie?" I suggest.

"Can't."

"Because you have a boyfriend?" That's what Gwen said. Joanne already has a boyfriend—all slow and deliberate so that I'd get it.

"No. Well, I did, but not anymore. Conrad. He's in Psych class with us."

"Oh, yeah. Unibrow Man. The Incrediblc Bulk."

"Very funny. He's a hockey player. But I broke up with him. So I'm free. Only Gwen doesn't want me seeing you."

"Why not?"

"She's afraid of you," she says. "Deer."

What? *Dear?*

"Deer, deer," she says, pounding my arm. "Stop."

I fishtail to a stop. At the side of the road is a deer. Her ears twitch, and then she leaps across the road, her white tail raised like a flag. That was close. Imagine the damage a deer might do to my car.

"Why is Gwen afraid of me?" I ask, getting back in gear.

"Her dreams." Jo claps her hand over her mouth. "Uh, oh."

I'm driving along a rock cut with a sheer wall of pink granite on my right and a drop-off of thirty feet on my left. I pretend the road is taking all my attention, but I'm thinking, *I knew it.* Gwen has some kind of special power.

"What dreams?" I ask, deliberately speaking in a casual tone.

"I can't tell you," Jo says.

"It'll be our little secret. I won't tell and you won't tell."

Jo sighs. "She gets dreams about what's going to happen."

"Like about the winning numbers for the lottery?"

I expect her to laugh, but she doesn't. She pulls on a piece of her hair, stares at it as if she wants to chew on the end, then lets it fall through her fingers. "She dreamed about you before you came. It's like there's some connection between you. She dreamed of fire, too, and coffins and a dead kid."

"The kid," I say. "He died in a fire, late Sunday night. My dad prepared the body."

"Yeah, well, Gwen thinks there's more to it than that. Thinks you're dangerous." She twists around to face me. "What happened today, Adrian? Did you really read Gwen's mind? What did you say to her when you ran after her?"

I stall for time. If I tell the truth, I'm screwed. Gwen will never talk to me, and, out of loyalty, Jo won't either. So I do the only thing I can do.

I lie.

"I'll let you in on a secret, Jo. The mind-reading thing? It's an act."

"But how'd you know about the scar?" she asks.

"Lucky guess." I wish I could read *Jo's* mind, but I can't. "Gwen was pretty upset by it, though. She said I was hard as stone."

"Stone," Jo says. "Grade eight. Stood her up for a date. He apologized a week later and asked her out, but she turned him down. I never understood that."

"And she still hates him?"

"He's symbolic, eh? Of all the times people put her down, called her names. She was the school loser."

"Why?" I ask.

"Easy target." Joanne shrugs. "A chunky monkey."

"Fat?"

"No, just short for her weight."

I look over to see if she's being funny on purpose. But her expression's serious and I can't tell.

"She wore braces," Joanne goes on, now chewing on a chunk of hair. "And glasses."

"Eighth grade was a long time ago, Jo," I say. "She needs to get over it."

"Sometimes you can't. People don't let you. It's a small school, Adrian. We've all known each other since JK."

"JK?"

"Junior kindergarten. It's like there's only so many parts to play. You know, class clown, class slut, geek, bimbo, loser. You missed the turn."

"Huh?" At first I think she's called me a loser for missing the turn. Then I realize she's switched gears again. We drive along in silence as I negotiate the twists in the road. I'm thinking about what she said, about labels. Growing up the son of a funeral director wasn't easy. Half the reason I took up weight lifting was to intimidate the guys who picked on me.

We arrive. "Thanks for the ride," Jo says.

"Anytime," I say. "Uh, Jo, I'm sorry I pulled that mind-reading stunt on Gwen. I guess it wasn't very funny."

"Yeah. Nobody laughed." Her eyes aren't so warm anymore.

"I'll make it up to her. I promise." This time I actually mean it.

But not for the reason Jo thinks.

Gwen

Had he read my mind? Impossible. But something weird had happened. When he touched me, the sudden jolt of energy caught me by surprise. It was like hot and cold and fire and ice all at once.

And it left me hungry. Ravenously hungry. I thought about grabbing a salad at Slim Fixings.

Forget that. I wanted *food*. I pulled through the Burger Barn drive-through and ordered a Monster Barn Burger with fried onions, bacon, and cheese, and a chocolate milkshake. I drove to Lakefront Park and parked the car facing the lake.

The wrapping around my burger crinkled as I unfolded it. The smell of grease and meat filled the car. Melted cheese and fried onions dripped down as I devoured the burger. I licked the onions off the now transparent wrapper, wishing there were more.

What's come over me?

It was as if the standoff with Adrian had awakened an enormous appetite in me. Or maybe I'd always been hungry but had denied it.

I burped, sucked up the last of my milkshake, and took a minute to enjoy the view. Out on the lake, the sky took up half the world. Nearly indigo above, it faded to light blue at the horizon. It reminded me of my dream. A wolf, stalking deer across the lake. I looked to my right, and there they were. Five deer, coming out of the nearest bay.

I clicked off several shots, capturing the deer's blue-black shadows on the white snow. Then the wolf appeared. He slunk along, freezing whenever a deer looked back. Finally, one deer broke into a run, alarming the others. His cover blown, the wolf turned back to shore.

I checked my shots. Perfect! I bet I could make the cover page.

Maybe the dreams weren't all bad.

THURSDAY, JANUARY 9

Adrian

People are vulnerable because of their needs. It's the flaw in their armor. Find the weakness, and one arrow can bring them down.

Like Jo. She needs to be taken seriously. That's why she joined the Debate Team and not the Cheerleading Squad. The armor-piercing arrow would be to call her an airhead. I'd nearly blown it by asking if she was a cheerleader. I wouldn't make that mistake twice.

Or Melissa. Throws herself at guys, sleeps around. All

she wants is someone to see past her body, to love her for herself. That's why the line, "He didn't give you the love and attention you deserve," worked so well on her.

And Gwen. What's her vulnerability? She hasn't gotten over being a loser. A "chunky monkey," as Jo put it. So what does she want? A guy who will worship her. Publicly. She wants every girl in the school to envy her.

So I'll give her what she wants. I'll do anything to feel that rush of power again. At the beginning of my lunch hour, I run out to a florist on Main Street.

"I need a single red rose," I tell the man behind the counter.

"Excellent choice." He gives me the once-over in a way that makes me uncomfortable. "You're in love."

"Not exactly."

"Oh, dear me. Then you might be giving the wrong message. A single red rose is a declaration of love. A single yellow rose means friendship. A pink rose—"

I cut him off. "How do you say you're sorry?"

"A lover's spat? Well, then. Nothing says 'forgive me' like a purple hyacinth."

"Good. Give me one of those."

He disappears into the back of the store, returning shortly with an armload of dark green spiky things. I guess he sees the look on my face.

"They're actually quite lovely when they bloom," he explains.

"I'll take your word for it." I pay for the plant and leave.

When I return to school, I find Gwen sitting alone,

reading the local paper. On the front page is a photo of deer being stalked by a wolf.

I set the pot of purple hyacinths on top of the photo. Gwen jerks back, startled, as if the green leaves were laced with poison. *It was a rose in my dream. What's this? The dream lied?*

Like Jo said. Precognitive dreams. Gwen's some kind of psychic energy magnet.

"I want to apologize," I tell her.

Her anger hits me like a spike driven into my brain. I hide my reaction. If she thinks I'm reading her mind, she'll run.

"I lied to you." Pain buffets me. "Look, I was wrong. I'm sorry."

Her expression softens. The pain lessens and I can breathe again. "Mind if I sit? I feel as if I'm on display." She glances over at the next table, where Melissa and her friends stare with their mouths open. She nods and I sit down.

"It's purple hyacinth, for forgiveness," I say, pointing to the plant.

He forgives me? For what? The nerve of him saying he—

And pain comes again, blood-red and pulsing.

"Gwen." I struggle to speak. "Will you listen for a second?"

"You've got one second." She's not smiling.

"It was all an act," I say.

"An act? How'd you know about the scar?" she demands.

"I've pried burgers apart like that myself. I have a little nick, right in that exact spot."

"The Crazy Glue. There's no way you could have guessed that."

"There are no stitch marks on either side of your scar. The Crazy Glue was a lucky guess. I was as surprised as you that I got it right."

She wavers. "But in the parking lot—you were so convincing. I thought for sure you were reading my mind."

"Body language, little signals. I've been pretending to read minds for years. You get good at making guesses, following hunches."

Like me. He's a Watcher like me? Reads body language. It's possible.

"Why? Why the act?"

"Why not?" I shrug. "Girls usually fall for it. Besides, it's easier than being myself."

Like me. Like Gwen-the-Photographer.

There's just enough truth in my statement that she believes me. Man, but I'm good!

"Could we start over again?" I give her my best puppy-dog look and she melts. I can see, in her mind, that she likes the fact that Melissa is staring at us. It's working!

I lift an eyebrow, tilt my head, and smile. I've practiced that move in the mirror. It never fails.

Another act? But he is cute.

Good. She's half mine already. Now, pay her a compliment.

"You have beautiful eyes. Don't hide them," I reach out and remove her glasses. Touching her, I feel the world come into sharper focus. Sounds louder. Colors brighter. Emotions more intense.

She hesitates, wondering if she can trust me. *He's flattering me. What does he want?*

And then it happens, *blam*, like a door opening in my mind. I'm suddenly hearing voices, like Gwen's mental voice, only not as strong. They rush into my head, competing for my attention, turning into shreds of sentences, dislocated phrases, half-heard words:

—*what's with the plant*

—*so intense, like they don't care they're in the cafeteria or*

—*what's he see in her, anyway?*

I let go of her hand, but the voices are still there.

—*Math test next period didn't study so screwed*

—*ooh nice nail color wonder if it's*

"What's wrong?" Gwen asks. *Looks like he's going to faint.*

"Migraine." I get up, nearly fall over.

"Maybe you should lie down." Gwen says.

"Good idea." I need to get away from her.

I stagger out of the cafeteria. Away from Gwen, the voices aren't as intense. But they're still there. I stumble down the hallway, heading blindly for the first-aid room. Along the way, a girl passes by. Her perfume jangles my nerves like loud music. I see a poster on a locker and it screams like a set of brakes worn down to the rotors. I hear a door slam and my vision fragments into broken glass.

My brain circuits are scrambled.

I find the first-aid room, babble "migraine" and "ice packs." An older woman takes my hand, leads me to a bed, brings ice, and draws the blinds.

The last thing I hear before I pass out is, *"Poor kid. White as a sheet."*

Only I hear it with my *mind.*

Gwen

In my dream, he gave me a rose—deep red, delicate, its petals barely beginning to open. But there I was, staring at a, what did he say it was? A purple hyacinth?

I turned the pot of green shoots around, looking more closely. In the middle of the clump was a knobby thing, like a small artichoke. I stared at it, struggling with my mixed feelings.

I can't trust him. He's a phony and a liar. He admitted it himself.

On the other hand, that way he has of tilting his head and smiling. Does he know what effect he has on a girl?

Get a grip. Of course he knows. He probably practices in the mirror.

But the way he'd looked at me, with hunger in his eyes, gave me shivers. And I had to admit, I loved the way Melissa gaped. Like why's the new hot guy talking to Gwen-the-Loser? Maybe Gwen's not a loser. Ha!

Your eyes are beautiful. Don't hide them.

Is that what I've been doing? Hiding? Behind my glasses, behind bulky sweatshirts, behind my camera?

After school, I stopped at the optometrist's office and left with a trial pair of green-tinted contact lenses. Next, clothes. Jeans, slung low on my hips. Tops, slinky, clingy with plunging necklines. Then, the big one. My hair.

"Chop it off," I said to the hairdresser. "Chin length.

Give me bangs. And let's do something about the color."

An hour later, I examined the results in the mirror. Short, bouncy, and very red. A perfect match for my green eyes.

I headed for the bakery to show Mom. She was placing a tray of apple strudel in the display case when I walked in. She brushed her hands on her white apron, and said, "May I help you?"

Then, "Oh, my gosh. Gwen? Your hair! Oh my goodness. Your eyes are *green!*"

"What do you think?"

"Well, it's quite a change," she said, frowning.

She didn't like it. I hadn't expected she would. Mom hates change. If the grocery store is out of her favorite tea, she'll spend ten minutes trying to choose another one. Sometimes she'll simply leave, too overwhelmed to decide.

"I was about to take a coffee break," Mom said.

"Okay." I followed her into the staff room. She put on fresh coffee, set out cream and sugar.

"Hungry?" she asked.

"No." I always said no. Then, "Wait, Mom. Yes. An éclair, please."

"Are you sure, honey? They're rather fa—uh, filling."

"I'm sure." Fattening, she was going to say.

She returned a second later with the éclair. Defiantly, I sank my teeth into the puff pastry, dark chocolate icing and rich cream filling. Ten seconds later, it was gone, leaving only sticky chocolate that I licked off the tips of my fingers.

"Goodness," said Mom. "What's come over you?"

"A zest for life," I said.

Mom smiled uncertainly, as if she wasn't sure about *zest*. She brought over two coffees. I stirred cream and sugar into mine. Mom left hers black and sipped carefully. She squinted at my hair.

"Why don't you come out and say it?" I said. "Tell me you hate it."

"Oh, honey, I don't hate it. It's just rather dramatic, don't you think?" she asked, smoothing back her own hair, now more gray than brown.

Well, if she thought that was dramatic, she certainly wouldn't like my new clothes. I kept my coat zipped up.

Mom took out her knitting and filled the small room with the chattering of her needles. I'd grown up with that sound. She must have knitted a hundred child-sized blankets for Emergency Services. Every cop car, ambulance, and fire truck in town carried a stash of them.

"Mom, why do you keep making those?" I asked, to make conversation. It was clear we wouldn't be talking about my transformation.

"Keeps my hands busy," she said.

My Watcher's instincts kicked in. Had there been the slightest hesitation in her voice, the briefest stutter in the smooth motion of her hands?

"Is that the only reason?"

Her hands stopped in mid-click. "Gwen, have you been talking to Aunt Grace? What did she tell you?"

Aunt Grace was Joanne's mother; my mom's sister.

"Oh, stuff," I lied. What was this? My mother had a *secret*?

Mom dropped her knitting. "I told her not to tell you.

What's done is done. Unless, oh, Gwen, tell me you're not getting them?"

"Getting them?"

"The dreams. Please tell me you aren't having them, too."

Too? My mother had the dreams? Is that why she's so timid, always looking back over her shoulder? *She* had the dreams?

I hesitated. I wanted to tell her, but I didn't want to worry her. Ever since Dad died, she'd been so fragile. In fact, she was fragile even before Dad died, leaving every decision up to him, even the little ones, like what to make for dinner.

"I don't know what you mean," I said. "What dreams?"

"So Grace didn't tell you. I made her promise."

"Mom, *what* dreams?"

"Ones that predict the future," Mom said.

"You had dreams like that?" I prompted.

"Oh, goodness. I guess you're old enough to know," Mom said. She picked up her coffee in both hands and gulped it down. "I was about your age. I'd met this boy, Matthew. He, oh, I'm sure you won't believe this, but if he touched something that was yours, he could tell things about you."

"Psychic," I said.

"Yes, I guess that's what you'd call it. And after I met him, I started having these dreams. Awful dreams. People dying. Accidents. A young girl, drowning out at Lakefront Beach. The mother asleep in the sun, the girl out on her air mattress. It had a leak, you see, and deflated. Matthew and I swam out, and brought her back to safety. The town gave us plaques for bravery. I still have mine."

"But, that's wonderful," I said.

"No, you don't understand. The girl died. Two weeks later. Pneumonia."

"The blankets," I said.

Mom gave me a knowing look. "The blankets. I couldn't save one child, but maybe I can comfort another."

"I'm sorry," I said, not sure what else to say. "Did you try to save anyone else?"

"There was no sense in trying. You can't change fate," Mom said. "The future is set in its course. It has its own momentum, like an avalanche. Once the snow breaks and starts to slide, there's nothing you can do until it's over."

Her voice trailed off. She stared into her empty cup as if it held an answer.

"What happened to Matthew?" I asked.

Mom shrugged. "He left, took a job up north. The dreams stopped. They never came back. A few years later, I met your father."

Did Matthew unlock some kind of latent ability in Mom? Is that what's happening to me?

"Gwen, are you okay?" Mom asked. "You are telling the truth, aren't you? You aren't having dreams like that, are you?"

"No, Mom," I assured her. "I guess you didn't pass them on."

"Thank goodness. Nothing good comes of them." She

reached across the table to pat my hand. "I have to get back to work. Be careful driving home, eh?"

"Yes, I'll be careful," I promised.

Sure, be careful, Gwen. Don't take risks. Watch life go by from the sidelines. And when a totally hot guy gives you a peace offering, hang back because you are afraid.

FRIDAY, JANUARY 10

Adrian

I'm driving home from school, but I'm thinking about yesterday.

I wake up in the first-aid room, headache-free and wondering if I'd only imagined my head cracking open. But then the first-aid volunteer asks how I am, and I hear, in my head, *looks better now.*

I'm buzzed, like I've eaten a bag of chocolate-covered coffee beans washed down with espresso. I want a friend, someone I can talk to. But there is no one. Being yanked up by the roots every few years means you don't make close friends. No one you can trust, anyway.

I dump my backpack at the front entrance. A fire crackles in the fieldstone fireplace. I smell pot roast and apple pie. I'm about to walk into the kitchen, when it happens again.

Dad: *Mrs. Neal at seven, go over arrangements, will need a lot of support. Prepare Mr. Neal later—wonder what dye might work best? Awfully sallow, after the cancer. Wait until morning? Nah. Tired, but I can manage.*

Mom: *He looks so tired. Shadows under his eyes. Taking on so much, running the place alone. Place called to him . . . so strange . . .*

I walk in. Mom lifts the lid off her slow cooker, looks around uncertainly for a place to put it.

Might mark the counter. Granite, though, shouldn't mark. So pretty.

She sets the lid on the top of the stove instead.

Dad watches her with a bemused smile. The smile fades as he looks at me.

"Your car start okay this morning?" he asks.

"Yeah," I answer.

"You're welcome," he says pointedly. *Never did thank me for paying for his block heater.*

"Uh, yeah. Thanks." Does he really have shadows under his eyes? Not sleeping well? Maybe it's guilt at dragging us along with him on his Great Canadian Adventure.

I grab a juice from the fridge, drain it, and set the bottle down on the kitchen counter.

"So, how was school?" Mom picks up the bottle, rinses it, and places it in the recycle bin under the sink. She wipes up the dark ring of moisture it left behind.

"The same. I went, I learned, I came home," I say. "I'm going down to do homework."

"I'll call you when dinner is ready," Mom says.

Dinner is quiet, with Dad not speaking except for "great roast" and "pass the potatoes." He leaves soon after, saying he has an appointment at the funeral home. I nearly say, *yeah, I know. Mrs. Neal,* but I keep my mouth shut. I clear the table and load the dishwasher, lost in my thoughts.

"Anything wrong?" Mom asks.

"Huh?"

She opens the microwave. There's the carton of milk I've just put away.

"Oops," I say.

Laugh lines crinkle around her eyes. Dad told me he married her for those eyes—clear gray and wide set. She places the milk in the fridge and waits.

"Do you believe in ESP?" I blurt out.

Mom wipes down the already clean counter and re-arranges a bowl of fruit. I catch myself tapping my fingers.

"What makes you ask?" she says.

I'm about to tell her, but two things stop me. One, I'm too old to run to my mother for advice. And two, I don't want her to know. Not yet, anyway. So I lie.

"We were talking about perception in Psych class and someone mentioned ESP."

Mom stalls, spraying and wiping off the appliances. "I

believe some people may connect with the world in a way most people cannot," she finally says.

"What do you mean?"

"Your father, for example. He has an uncanny ability to understand what other people are feeling. You could call it empathy, but it goes deeper than that. He can't separate himself from the pain of his clients. It takes its toll over time."

"Well, no offense, Mom, but I think Dad needs to let go a little. Stop taking on everyone's problems."

"He can't, Adrian. Every gift has a price."

A price? Yeah, I can see that. Like the pain in my head when Gwen cracked it open. But, man, the rush was great. And imagine how I can use this. Knowing what people are thinking? What could possibly be the drawback in that?

My thoughts return to the present as I pull into the parking lot. Walking into the school is like walking into a beehive. There's buzz all around me, and only I can hear it.

—*and then she sat down and I could see her thong, like oh man and*

—*equal to the sum of the square of the other two sides, equal to the*

—*1867, no wait, or was it 1876? Or maybe*

—*and then I said to him, I said*

—*only three days late, been that late before but*

I go into English class, sit down, try to ignore the voices in my skull. Suddenly it's like someone turned up the volume.

This girl walks in. Melissa? Same color hair, only

shorter. Same kind of clothes, tight jeans and a low-cut top with spaghetti straps.

Uh, oh. He's checking me out.

The voice appears in my head, full-blown, so much louder than all the other voices.

Gwen?

I can't believe it. She looks totally different. What has she done to her hair? But, man, the way she fills out a top is amazing.

"Hi," she says, sitting down beside me. *Oh, please, please let him say he likes my hair.*

"I love your hair," I say, lying through my teeth. I hate the hair. It's so *red*. And the contacts, so obviously fake, make her look cheap. But that's not what she wants to hear.

"Now your beautiful eyes are even more beautiful," I say, and feel a warm flush of pleasure from her.

When English ends, we go our separate ways. We meet again at lunch, and sit at our table. Jo walks in. When she sees Gwen, she squeals, loud enough that the whole cafeteria hears.

"Omigosh!" she gasps, sitting down. "Wow! I didn't believe it. I mean, everyone's talking about your hair, but I never thought you'd ever do it."

What Jo is thinking is: *everyone was right. It's hideous. Totally the wrong color for your skin tone. Whatever possessed you?* "I mean, *wow!*" she says again.

Tone it down already. People are staring, Gwen thinks.

"Let them stare," I say.

"What?" says Gwen.

Think fast. "Everyone's staring, Gwen," I say, trying to cover up my mistake. "You're beautiful."

She flushes.

She looks like Melissa, Jo is thinking.

"Yeah, that's what I thought," I say.

Gwen looks at me with suspicion. I'm screwing up big time.

I drop my voice down, bedroom-soft, and capture Gwen with my eyes. "That's what I always thought, Gwen, that you would be very pretty if you wore contacts."

Gwen's thoughts muddle. *What just happened?*

I take her hand, and her thoughts become even more jumbled. Then something weird happens. Gwen feels a momentary sense of vertigo, like the world shifted on its axis. A vision comes to her.

We are in my bedroom, backlit with candlelight. I'm standing behind her, my arms wrapped around her. She shivers, leans back so our bodies touch. We're facing the full-length mirror in my wardrobe. I could swear our eyes are glowing.

The vision ends. Gwen won't look at me. I feel her emotions. Fear and amazement and hope in equal parts. She's wondering, *what was that? A waking dream? A vision? I'm getting visions now?*

Yes, you *are* getting visions now, I want to tell her. Just as you opened a door in my mind, I have opened a door in yours.

SATURDAY, JANUARY 11

Gwen

Last night, over and over, I had the same dream. Us, in his bedroom, dozens of candles burning, his arms around me. It was the same as the vision I had when he touched my hand. Each time I awakened, not knowing what would happen next. But from the pounding of my heart, I could guess.

Was Mom right about the future? That it's set in its course, like an avalanche, rushing to its natural conclusion. But what conclusion is that? I think I already know.

* * *

This morning, right after dawn, I had a new dream. A grubby old guy had passed out in an alley.

I showered, then went downstairs and reached for my usual low-fat cereal and skim milk. The first bite made me retch. I tossed it out and made bacon and eggs instead. Now that my appetite was awake, it demanded to be satisfied. I topped off my breakfast with two pieces of toast and jam, then called Joanne.

"Hey. Were you asleep?"

"Of course not," she yawned.

"Good, I'm on my way," I said.

I hopped on our snowmachine and drove down our snow-covered lawn to the lake. Once on the ice, I cautiously puttered along.

Cautious. Like Mom.

I twisted my wrist, gunning the gas. The engine roared and the machine leaped forward. The wind, fiercely cold, whipped past me. I arrived at Joanne's to find her sitting at the breakfast counter, eating sausages and pancakes. Aunt Grace set down her pancake flipper and gave me a bear hug.

"Let me take a good look, Gwen." She walked around me in a circle, fluffing my hair with her hands. "Fabulous."

I couldn't be sure, but I got the feeling that she didn't actually like it, but didn't want to hurt my feelings.

Aunt Grace handed me a plate of pancakes and sausages, then left, saying, "I'll leave you two girls alone to gab now."

"So, why the change, Gwen?" asked Joanne, once Aunt Grace left the room. "Adrian?"

55

I drowned my pancakes in maple syrup before answering. "No, of course not. It was just time."

"Ha. Right." Joanne ran her finger over the syrup on her plate and brought it, dripping, to her mouth. "There's something weird going on, you know? Like you two are magnets, first repelling, then attracting."

I'm thinking of my vision, of us in his bedroom, his arms around me, our eyes glowing in the candlelight. I haven't told Joanne yet. I barely believe it myself.

"Um," I hesitated. "Joanne, do you like him?"

"Of course I like him. That's not the point."

"What is?"

"You got the dream. He came to you," Joanne said, for once completely serious.

That's ridiculous, I thought. Or was it? I finished my second breakfast, then said to Joanne. "Speaking of dreams, I've had another one. Some old drunk passed out in an alley."

"Whoohoo," said Joanne. "What are we waiting for?"

Adrian

Saturday morning, I wake up alone in my own head. Or almost alone. I feel a whisper of thought from my mother, downstairs, reading the paper. Dad must be at work already. I shower, gulp down a protein shake and tell Mom that I'm off to work at the funeral home.

First job, clear the walks. A foot of snow fell overnight. It's fresh powder with the consistency of dust. I dig a shovel in, lift, and throw. It slides sideways off my shovel, right back onto the path. After an hour, I'm soaked through with sweat, shivering in my leather coat, and cursing my father all over again.

I carry the shovel into the office, where Dad sits at his desk looking over a stack of files.

"This sucks," I inform him. Okay, maybe that's not the best way to say "good morning, dear father," but I'm not in my happy place.

He looks up. "You're dripping on my carpet."

"I need a snow blower," I reply.

He rifles through the newspaper and pushes a section toward me. "Can't afford it. Buy this instead."

This is a gigantic aluminum shovel called a "snow float." I'm not amused.

"And while you're at it," Dad goes on, "pick up a gallon of paint in this color." He reaches into his suit pocket and slides a paint chip across the desk.

"You're painting the bathroom?" The bathroom off the master bedroom is, in Mom's words, a "bilious yellow."

"Nope. You are."

"What? *No way!*"

"And who paid for your block heater?"

"When are you going to stop throwing that in my face? Look, I'll pay you back."

Stalemate. We face off, glaring, arms folded.

Dad breaks first. "You hate it here, don't you? I feel it. Your anger, your resentment." He uncrosses his arms, leans forward, clasps his hands together. "I lie awake at night,

Adrian, wondering what got into me. What was I thinking, uprooting you without a good reason?"

I realize something. It's not his fault. I think back to my mother's words: *your father felt compelled to move here. He felt you belonged here.* It had sounded bizarre at the time, but that was before I'd met Gwen.

"Uh, look, it's fine, Dad," I say. "It's working out."

He doesn't seem convinced. "Are you sure? You could go back to Milwaukee, live with Joel."

I just look at him. Joel, my older brother, is married with a baby on the way.

"Okay, not my best idea," Dad says. "Look, do you think we could get back on speaking terms?"

I nearly spill my guts, right then and there. Hey, Dad. Guard your thoughts, okay? I can read you like a book.

Bad move. So, what I say is, "Sure."

Then we look at each other. After thirty seconds of silence, we both break out into goofy grins.

"So, what's new?" Dad asks.

"Not much. What's new with you?" I reply.

We grin a bit longer, then Dad says, "Well, if you don't mind picking up that paint, I'll give you my debit card." *I should tell him to buy a winter jacket and warm boots. He must be freezing in that leather coat.*

"Hey, thanks," I say.

"Thanks?" *What just happened? What did Helen say? That he was asking her about ESP?*

"Uh, yeah. For the debit card." Oh, man, that was lame. Will he buy it?

"Oh," says Dad. *Nah. Mind reading's impossible.*

I suppress my sigh of relief. Don't blow it.

"By the way, why don't you look for a winter jacket and warm boots? You must be freezing in that leather coat of yours."

"Thanks!" I leave before I give myself away.

Gwen

We found him in the narrow alley beside the coffee shop. He wore a ratty brown coat and a gray hat, exactly like in my dream. The deep lines in his face were fuzzed with beard stubble. Clutched tightly in his hand was a whiskey bottle, half-concealed by a brown paper bag.

"Is he dead?" Joanne whispered.

"Well, if he is, we aren't going to disturb him by talking out loud," I whispered back.

"Funny, ha, ha. Go check."

"Why me?"

"It was *your* dream."

That was hardly logical, but I couldn't think of a good comeback. I ventured into the alley. Drifting snow partially covered the ground, along with chocolate-bar wrappers, fast-food containers, and broken beer bottles.

"Check his pulse," Joanne said.

I crouched down. Even in the frigid air, I could smell him.

"Hey, Joanne," I called. "Can lice jump?"

She grimaced and made an impatient "go on" gesture.

As I reached toward him, he blew out a loud, reverberating fart.

"He's alive," I said, holding my nose. I grabbed my camera.

"What are you doing?" Joanne asked.

"Well, you see, when I push this button here," I said, demonstrating, "I get this image of whatever I'm looking at."

"Very funny. You can't print a picture of him. How would his family feel?"

"If they're that concerned, they ought to take care of him," I argued. Just the same, I clapped the lens cap back on my camera and put it away. Maybe Joanne was right. I didn't need to exploit the old guy's misery.

I pulled out my phone instead and dialed 411. "Hi, I need the number for the Rocky Water Police, please."

The operator gave me the number. "Should I connect you?"

I hesitated. The future is set in its course. *But not today.*

"Yes, please connect me."

Adrian

I drive through silence. Snow-covered road, empty woods. No voices in my head. This ends when I arrive in town. I walk into Canadian Tire, looking for paint and a snow float. It's Saturday and it's a big store and it's filled with people.

The mental noise deafens me. I grab a snow float, pick up a gallon of paint, and take it to the counter to get the color mixed in.

"You want this shook up?" asks the paint guy. He's about my age, with spiked blue hair and a tongue stud. He puts the paint can into a mixer. Above the racket, I hear his thoughts—*hurts to pee. Burns like*—

As if I need this. Then, another voice speaks in my head.

—*morning sunrise or peach delight? Morning sunrise . . . better with the drapes . . . too pink . . . but the peach is too peachy . . . might clash with the rug . . .*

I look beside me to see a middle-aged woman agonizing over two paint samples. Behind me, a baby, bundled up to its eyeballs in a snowsuit, hat, mittens, and a blanket, sits fussing in his car seat. His mental whining cuts through my head like a table saw.

I pay for the paint, say to the guy with the blue spikes, "See your doctor." I turn to the middle-aged woman beside me and say, "Morning Sunrise," then say to the mother of the fussy baby, "He's hot."

Then I leave. I'm partway out of the store when I hear another voice.

Can lice jump? It sounds like Gwen. I jerk my head around, looking for her, but she isn't there.

Could I be hearing her from a distance? Still wondering, I walk the few blocks over to First Street. A police car drives by and stops. Two uniformed cops walk into an alley and reappear half-carrying some old drunk. They pour him into the back of the police car and leave.

Nice town.

I walk into a store advertising a sale. Everything's twenty-five percent off. One look tells me I've come to the right place. Jackets crowd the racks. One entire wall is overed with hats and gloves and something labeled "neck warmers." They look like fleece tubes.

"Need some help?" asks a girl with a freckled nose and brown eyes.

"Yeah. I need some warm clothes."

She gives my leather coat the once-over. "Come with me. I'll take care of you."

I see in her mind that she'd like to take care of me in more ways than one. Before long, I'm looking at a stack of stuff beside the cash register—a parka and boots guaranteed to keep me warm to forty below, insulated gloves, and a neck warmer.

The girl, Mandy, rings up the sale. I whistle when I see the total.

"You could wait until next week," suggests Mandy. "Everything's half off then."

"How about giving me half off now?" I give her my best little-boy smile.

"I couldn't." *Boss is on holiday. She'd never know.*

"No one will know," I push. "It'll be our little secret."

She wavers. *She'd never find out. Never checks my sales receipts.*

"I won't tell and you won't tell," I say, dropping my voice down into seduction range. I slip around the counter, move in close. "Don't make me beg, Mandy."

He's adorable. Wonder how he kisses?

I look around the store. We're alone. I lead her behind a rack of clothes. I draw out the moment, moving in close, leaning down so our lips almost touch. I pull back to give her time to say no.

I must be crazy, she thinks. *I don't even know him. Oh, no. Don't leave. Do it. Do it, already.*

I mean to kiss her lightly, a mere brush of my lips on

hers, but she leans into me and gives me a long, slow kiss. I break away first.

"Wow," she says.

"Yeah, wow," I say. "So, about that discount?"

She hesitates, then, "Sure."

I pay with Dad's debit card and tell her thanks.

"Wait." She scribbles her number on a piece of paper and hands it to me. "Call me."

"I will," I promise, as the door chimes on my way out.

But I know I won't. She got what she wanted. I got what I wanted. End of transaction; both parties satisfied.

Gwen

After calling the police, I left Joanne sipping a latte at Freshly Ground and headed over to the newspaper office, where Doug was on weekend coverage.

"Hey, kiddo," Doug said. "Nice hair. So what brings you in on a Saturday?"

"I've been thinking about that fire. I'd like to do a background article about arson. You know, typical profile, motivation, common methods. That sort of thing."

"What? A week ago, you said you were a photographer, not a reporter," said Doug.

"Things change," I said. "So, can I go ahead?"

"Hmm, I don't know," said Doug, pushing his sleeves up. "We don't want to run anything that could be seen as sensationalism."

"You could hold it until the guy strikes again," I said.

"*When?*"

"*If* he strikes again."

Doug cracked his knuckles. I held my breath.

"Okay. Go for it."

"Thanks, Doug. You won't regret this."

He shook his head as if bemused. "You know, kiddo, you've got good instincts. You'll make a fine reporter."

I grinned all the way back to Freshly Ground.

SUNDAY, JANUARY 19

Adrian

A week passes. I learn something. There are pluses and minuses to reading minds.

On the plus side, it can be useful. When I don't know the answers on an English quiz, I borrow them from Gwen's head. In History, I'm zoning out when the teacher asks me a question. The answer is in his mind. On Monday, I see that my mother is planning to cook liver and onions for dinner. I grab a burger on my way home.

On the minus side, I have very little control over what

comes into my head. It's like walking through an electronics store with every stereo, every television turned up at max volume. Working for Dad at the funeral home is killing me, no pun intended.

Normally, my job is easy: greet people at the door, direct them to the right rooms, make sure there's always hot coffee, keep the walks clear of snow. But, one night, we have a visitation for the family of a suicide. He's young, only sixteen. His mother's grief is so raw that I find myself locked in the bathroom, my heart racing, my stomach churning. I turn on the tap, splash water over my face. I'm shaking so violently that I can barely grab a paper towel. I have to gain some control over this. No way will I turn into my father.

How do you control your own mind? Weight lifting helps, but only while I'm working out. So, feeling a bit foolish, I give meditation a try. I light a single candle and stare at the flame. I block out everything, even my own thoughts. After several nights, I achieve stillness. I try to remember that stillness at school, when Gwen's presence magnifies everything. I can't block completely, but at least I am able to lower the volume.

And so the week passes, each day revolving around Gwen. On Monday, she leaves for her newspaper job full of excitement. She's working on a story about the arsonist. One phrase repeats in her head, *you've got good instincts*. She loves the sound of it.

Meanwhile, she's still suspicious of me. Had I lied? Am I reading her mind? Invading her privacy? She tests me, imagining gross images and watching for my reaction. On Tuesday, I'm about to bite into a tuna sandwich when she thinks about maggots, forty or fifty fat, glistening, white maggots, crawling over the surface of my sandwich. I bite into the sandwich and smile. On Thursday, I pick up my carton of milk. She imagines sour milk: pale liquid filled with chunks. I drain the entire carton and continue on with our conversation. I can almost feel the chunks sliding down my throat; can almost taste the vile liquid.

It's a game with shifting rules. She's sneaky and under-handed. I respect that. I like a challenge. Besides, I have my own secret weapon.

Flowers.

On Monday, I bring her a yellow rose. My florist guy gives me a card, and I write a single word on it: Friendship.

On Tuesday, I give her Baby's Breath: For Innocence.

Wednesday, I bring a yellow daffodil. I write on the card: The sun shines when I am with you.

Thursday, a pink camellia. I am longing for you.

And on Friday, phlox. I don't even know what phlox is, but I'm going on the advice of my new friend, the florist. I write on the card: Our souls are united.

Gwen smiles.

Gwen

I think he was telling the truth about not reading my mind. I tested him a few times by imagining the grossest images I could imagine. He didn't react. Not even an involuntary shudder. I imagined maggots on his sandwich and he bit into it with obvious enjoyment. Sour milk, and he swallowed it without hesitation. No one has that kind of self-control. As a Watcher, I'm sure of this. There would have been some small sign if he'd seen the images in my mind.

We sit together in English and in Psychology. He has lunch with me every day. When Joanne joins us, he is polite, but he gives his attention to me.

I discover things about him. I'm pop or soft rock; he's alternative rock. I'm Russian novels; he's classic cars and body-building magazines. I'm quiche and spinach salad; he's steak, rare, with a Caesar salad on the side.

But we have some things in common. Movies set in the Middle Ages, knights and chivalry and stealing from the rich to give to the poor. And anything supernatural—movies, TV shows, even books, though he reads only graphic novels.

And then, there's the flowers. I thought it was dumb that Conrad brought Joanne flowers, but now I'm waiting to see what each new day will bring. I love the way he writes a message for each one, love the way he brushes against me as he hands me the flower. Love the intensity of his blue eyes and the way he looks into mine as if he has nothing else in the world to do.

The weirdest thing happens when we touch. I feel that warmth, that tingle, running through me. Everything seems sharper, clearer. Often a vision comes to me.

The arsonist will strike again. That's a recurring vision. Where or when, I don't know, but it feels like it might be soon. And when it does, Doug will run my background article. He's already read it and pronounced it, "Excellent work. Good, objective reporting." I'm hoping, if I can impress him, that I can land a summer internship at the paper. How cool would that be?

Adrian

On Sunday, I'm painting the master bathroom when I learn another price of my gift.

Dad pokes his head around the corner. "Hey, guy, how's it going?"

"Fine."

"Missed some." Dad points.

I slide the roller over the spot. Paint speckles fly through the air, making a splatty sound.

"Yup, this is going to look great," says Dad. "Terrific house, don't you think?"

"Um-hmm." I'm concentrating, trying not to get paint on the woodwork.

"Great bathroom, too," Dad rambles on. "Great big Jacuzzi tub, huge shower."

I freeze. I'm reading his thoughts. He's thinking of that nice big shower, big enough for two people. *Oh, man.* They went at it, last night, right there in the shower. I see the memory in Dad's mind. Sick. It's like watching porn, *only it's my parents.*

"Uh, Dad? You have to leave."

"Huh?"

"I've got to, uh, use the . . . " I motion toward the toilet.

"Oh! Sure! Catch you later."

I drop the paint roller into the pan, lock the door, sink to the floor. The room spins. There are certain things I don't need to know, and this is at the top of the list. I leave without bothering to clean up. A moment later, I'm in my car, heading to town, driving on autopilot. I wind up at the school. The whole time I'm telling myself, I can control this mind-reading thing. Dad caught me off guard, that's all.

I'm caught up in my own thoughts. Then I hear a voice that isn't my own. *It's happening.*

It's Gwen. I tune in on her and see the image of a train barreling down the tracks, smashing into a pickup truck. I focus, pull in the details. It's the tracks near school, a few blocks away.

Gwen

"**A**re you sure about this?" Joanne asked.

"Not totally sure. The dreams aren't that specific." I'm thinking about the rose that became a hyacinth.

"Great," said Joanne. "You drag me out of bed with some story about a train wreck, freeze my butt off waiting in your car for four hours, and now you tell me *you aren't sure?*"

"All I know is that a train will come around that bend," I said, pointing, "at the same time as a red pickup decides to run the barrier. I don't know if it will happen in the next five seconds, or the next five hours, or the next five days."

"Great. Meanwhile, we starve," grumped Joanne.

"There's a granola bar in the glove compartment."

Joanne grabbed it, ripped off the wrapper.

"Give me half," I said.

"I liked you better before," Joanne said, cramming her half of the granola bar into her mouth.

I ate mine quickly, before she could demand more than her share. I closed my eyes, remembering the details of my dream: the train, its brakes screaming, whistle blowing. It hits the truck, sending it flying off the tracks. The truck comes to rest in a tangle of crumpled metal.

Joanne brought me back to reality by pounding on my arm. "Gwen. Truck, truck!"

"It's happening," I said.

Parked at the top of a hill, we could clearly see the scene below. The barrier arms lowered; the red warning lights blinked. The train rounded the bend, obscured by the ice fog that had collected in the valley. From our height, we could see the train. From the tracks, the driver of the truck would see only fog.

"Hey, we gotta warn him," Joanne yelled, wrenching open the car door. She ran down the hill toward the tracks.

The air *shifted* around me. A new vision came.

The truck is thrown off the tracks, sails through the air. Joanne has time to scream once before it smashes into her.

"Joanne, no!" She was halfway down the hill.

From behind me, I heard footsteps. Adrian. He flew past me, reached Joanne and pushed her aside. A snowbank caught her fall.

"What the—?" she gasped.

Adrian took off his coat, waved it frantically at the truck.

The truck ducked under the first barrier arm just as it lowered. The train bore down, its whistle blowing, brakes squealing. The driver of the truck hit the gas and burst through the second barrier. The train roared by a split second later.

Safe.

I glanced down at my shaking hands, surprised to see I was holding my camera. When had I grabbed it? How many pictures had I taken? I ran down the hill to where Joanne was brushing snow off her coat and spluttering.

"You okay?" I asked.

"Yeah, thanks to Adrian," she said, giving him a hug that nearly knocked him off his feet.

I suppressed a jab of jealousy and joined the hug-fest, wrapping my arms around them both. Over Joanne's head, Adrian gave me a big smile.

"You going to get his name or anything?" Adrian asked, nodding toward the pickup truck.

"Oh," I said. "Yeah."

What was I thinking? I felt like my head was floating free.

"You okay?" I asked the guy in the truck.

He tugged on the brim of his red baseball cap and nodded. "*Hooeee,* that was close. Good thing that young man waved his coat at me. I didn't see no train coming. Hidden by the fog, eh?"

"Yes, good thing," I said. "I'm from the *Rocky Waters Press*. Could I have your name?"

"For the paper? Sure. James Dean. Like the actor." He let out a "heh-heh-heh" kind of laugh. "The wife'll flip when she sees it. Keeps telling me not to run that barrier. How's my front grill?"

I took a look. "Dented."

"Well, yeah, could have been a lot worse. Could have gotten killed, eh?"

Not just you, I thought. *Joanne, too.*

Adrian

James Dean, like the actor. She writes down the name, then tries to put the lens cap back on her camera, but her hands are shaking too much. I take the camera, cap it, hand it back. Her eyes are filled with tears.

So close. Could have killed her.

On impulse, I wrap my arms around her. She resists for a second, then leans into me. Her tears wet my new jacket. From beside us, I hear Jo say, very quietly, "What did I tell you? Magnets."

Gwen calms down and, as she does, her suspicions reappear. *How did he know the train would hit Joanne? Maybe he lied to me about not reading my mind. Maybe he's been reading it all along.*

Think fast. I shift my head toward Jo. "What were you thinking, running so close to the tracks? Didn't you hear Gwen scream at you?"

Jo stammers. "I, uh, wasn't thinking straight, I guess."

That satisfies Gwen, but then she asks, "How'd you manage to show up in the nick of time?"

"I came into town to pick up some paint. I saw your car."

She notices a smear of blue on my face and she believes my lie. The wind whips her hair across her face. I gently push it aside with one hand, but keep my other arm tight around her. She forgets to be suspicious. A dozen emotions whirl in her head, like she's hit the frappe button on a blender.

So close to her, touching her, I feel the energy run through her and into me. All I want is to be near her, to feel The Power sing in my head and flow through my veins.

She feels it, too. Feels my energy moving into her and through her. It thaws her from the inside out, until even her fingers, icy from using her camera, tingle with warmth.

It scares her, makes her want to pull away, but in the next second, she gives in. Linked to her mind, maybe I give in as well. Our breathing goes shallow, our hearts beat faster, the palms of our hands grow damp. I tilt my head down, coming close to kissing her. Then I stop. Take it slow. Don't frighten her.

A vision hits her.

It starts out as before: us, in my bedroom, candles lit, my arms around her, her leaning back into me. But, then it shifts. We are kissing; the kind of kissing that can only lead to one thing.

That's when I know I've played my cards right.

Gwen

Had I been wrong about him?

After his almost-kiss, I grabbed a burger, then raced over to the newspaper office. I kept remembering his lips, nearly touching mine and then pulling away. The air between us had felt charged. I'd felt a rush of energy run through me, warming every part of me.

And the vision. It was all I could think about. What did it mean? Him, with me? Impossible. The fat girl never gets the guy.

Enough, I thought. Focus. Get back to work.

I downloaded my shots into my computer, chose six of the best, then reviewed them before e-mailing them to Doug. They were all of Adrian. Adrian pulling Joanne out of harm's way. Adrian waving his jacket at the truck. Adrian talking to the driver.

Was I going soft in the head? I made another selection, making sure I had several of the truck jumping the tracks, crashing through the barrier, with the train a blur in the background. I left one of Adrian, the one where he was waving his coat in the air.

I kept the rest for myself.

MONDAY, JANUARY 20

Adrian

I wake up with gut pains that come in waves. I get Mom to call me in sick, then go back to bed. By eleven, I'm slept out. I'm not any better, but I'm no worse. I pick up a flower for Gwen, then head over to the school in time for lunch.

Balancing a bowl of soup and some crackers, I walk over to Gwen's table. I hold out the flower. From one table over, I hear Melissa's thoughts: *Are they going out now? What does he see in her?*

I look at Gwen and what I see is a great body, shown off by

a tight sweater, a short skirt and matching boots. And what I feel is the energy, The Power that flows in her like a river.

She takes the flower from me.

"A blue camellia," I explain.

"Where's the card?"

"No card this time," I say, leaning in close and dropping my voice so only she can hear. "It means: you are a flame in my heart."

Her face turns pink. She runs the tip of one finger over the soft petal of the flower, caressing it. I imagine those fingers, touching me the way she touches the flower, all feathery light.

My jeans are suddenly too tight. I shift, trying to get comfortable. Then a cramp hits me, killing the urge.

"Hey, Adrian. You look awful," Jo says, joining us at the table.

"Probably something I ate." Another cramp hits and I am manly enough not to groan. But at that exact moment, Gwen *does* groan.

Should have taken something for this. Uh, oh, leakage alert.

"Be right back," Gwen says. *Don't want to ruin this skirt.*

She leaves. Jo looks at me closely, says, "You sure you're all right, Adrian?"

I nod, too horrified to speak. I'm linked to Gwen. I feel what she feels. Period cramps.

And I can't block her.

Gwen

After lunch, I drove over to the newspaper. I took the camellia in with me, not wanting it to freeze in my car.

"Awww, sweetheart, you shouldn't have," said Doug, as I entered his office.

"Oh, uh, I didn't, I mean . . . " I stammered.

"Relax, kiddo," said Doug. A grin lifted the corners of his eyes. "Secret admirer?"

"Sort of."

"About time. Look, I want to talk to you about this." One stubby finger tapped the surface of a photo on his ink blotter. My picture, I saw, of the truck smashing through the barrier.

What's wrong? It's a great image.

Doug leaned back and crossed his long arms over his barrel chest. "So, what's the story, kiddo?"

"Well, I, uh, just happened to be there and—"

"Yeah, yeah. Who is this guy?"

"Mr. Dean."

"That much I know. I read your cutline, Gwen." He tapped a few keys on his keyboard, using the hunt-and-peck method. He read off the screen: "A Rocky Waters resident, Mr. James Dean, narrowly escaped injury while crossing the tracks on Eighth Street early Sunday morning."

"I'm sorry—" I started to say.

Doug waved his hand, cutting me off. "So what? Instincts asleep? I thought you were a reporter."

I sat there, stunned. Doug was right. In all the excitement, I'd forgotten to get the story. I'd been too awestruck by the visions, coming one on top of each other. Too frantic that I'd put Joanne in danger. Too caught up in Adrian's embrace.

This was no way to earn a summer internship.

"I'll have the story on your desk by the end of the day," I promised.

Doug nodded, waved his hand for me to go. Back at my computer, I went online and pulled up Mr. Dean's number. It wasn't hard to find. There was only one James Dean in town.

I dialed the number. "Hello? I'm Gwen from the *Rocky Waters Press*. I took Mr. Dean's photo yesterday? Is Mr. Dean there, please?"

"Oh, my," said an elderly woman on the other end. I heard her call out, "Jimmy? Jimmy, phone for you. It's a *reporter!*"

SATURDAY, JANUARY 25

Adrian

Gwen's story runs in the Tuesday paper. She says it's no big deal, but I can sense her excitement. Her editor gives her half a page. He uses three photos—the pickup crashing through the barrier, a close-up of Mr. Dean, and one of me, waving my coat and pointing down the track.

We sit together at lunch, alone, but we are interrupted half a dozen times. People congratulate us. We're celebrities, and Gwen looks the part. She's wearing khaki pants and a black top laced in the front. My eyes keep wandering from her face down to those laces.

I tap into people's thoughts. Most of them figure we're going out together. They've stopped wondering what I see in her. Her approval rating soars. I catch Stone looking at her. I mean *really* looking at her. Thinking about how her breasts would feel in his hands. I nearly go over there and break all his fingers. But I don't. I've got more control than that. And how would I explain it to Gwen? That I read Stone's mind? Yeah, that would go over well. Besides, it doesn't matter how much Stone fantasizes. She's mine. Or, at least, she will be soon.

On Friday, our English teacher announces we'll begin studying Shakespeare next week.

I groan.

"What's wrong?" Gwen whispers to me.

"Oh, nothing. Shakespeare, Greek, Latin, Swahili—all the same to me."

She grins. I see in her mind that she loves Shakespeare. It's her second language. Well, maybe third. English and French came first.

"Uh, Gwen, would you be willing to help me study?" I give her my best little-boy smile and she melts.

"Sure."

"How about coming over to my house on Saturday night?" I suggest. "My parents are going to Winnipeg for the weekend. We'll be able to work undisturbed."

She hesitates. In her mind is the vision. Us. In my bedroom. Kissing. She remembers my words: *You are a flame in my heart.*

"Okay," she agrees.

I read her mind. We both know we aren't going to study.

Gwen

All day long, my stomach knotted up. Was I crazy? I hardly knew him. I showered, and checked myself in the mirror, trying to be objective.

Breasts, my best feature. Or, is that features?

Waist. It curves in. Not much, but it *does* curve in.

Belly. Curves out. Michelangelo would have loved to paint me. Oh, well, I can suck it in. If I give up breathing.

Hips. Wide. A baby machine. A plus. Ummm, actually not sure about that one.

Thighs. Forget the thighs.

Who am I kidding? He couldn't possibly want me. *But the vision.* It will happen, because I *saw* it happen.

"I'm going over to Adrian's to study now," I told Mom.

"Be careful," she warned.

"I will," I promised, grabbing my snowmachine gear. The night was clear. The stars shed just enough light to lead me to Adrian's. I knew the way. I'd babysat at that house countless times.

I parked at his dock and walked up. Like so many houses on the lake, it was built into the hillside, with a lower level walk-out from the family room. Golden light spilled out of the glass doors, like sunshine saved from summer. Wood smoke, sweet and welcoming, hung in the still air.

Adrian opened the door. A tiny piece of tissue clung to his chin, where he'd cut himself shaving. He looked gorgeous, and smelled even better.

"Uh, you, uh . . . ." I stammered, pointing to his chin.

"Oh." He removed the tissue. "Better?"

"Actually, I thought it was cute," I said.

"Cute? A man nearly slices his neck open trying to clean up for his lady, and you think it's cute?"

He spoke in a low, teasing voice that sent shivers through me. *His lady*. I liked that. He reached out to unzip my snowmachine suit.

"Uh, that's okay," I said, fumbling for the zipper.

Lit only by the glow of fire in the woodstove, the family room felt intimately small. From my vision, I recognized the overstuffed couch, the weight equipment in an alcove to the right, Adrian's bedroom straight ahead.

What am I doing? This is so not me. I should go.

"Second thoughts?" Adrian asked, head tilted. He stood outlined by the flickering light of the woodstove, waiting.

"I'm good," I said.

He took my hand, and led me to his room.

I'm not sure what I expected. My vision showed an old-fashioned wardrobe and candles. That was it. I looked around, trying to find the right word for his room. Uncluttered? Army-neat?

No, the right word was *austere*. Dark carpet, light walls, black furniture, a gray comforter on his bed. There were no mementos, no souvenirs, no photographs. It was as if he'd passed through life without connecting to anyone or anything. The only decorations, if you could call them that, were a sword and a dagger mounted on his wall.

"It's my hobby, medieval weaponry," Adrian said. "This is a replica of the sword thought to be that of Edward the Black

Prince, son of Edward the Third, father of Richard the Second."

He drew the sword out of its black scabbard. It was easily a meter long, with a blade that tapered to a wickedly sharp tip.

"Want to try it?" he asked.

"No, thanks." It looked deadly.

Adrian replaced the sword and took down the dagger. "This then? It's a parrying dagger, based on one carried in around 1580 by the bodyguard of the Elector of Saxony."

The dagger fit neatly in my hand, the leather handle smooth, the grooved blade shining softly.

"Beautiful, isn't it?" Adrian said. "Engraved pommel, hardwood grip, covered in leather, a ring guard to protect your knuckles, fullered blade made of cold, hard steel."

"Yes," I agreed, turning it over to catch the light on the blade.

"There's something seductive about it, isn't there?" Adrian went on. "The power of life and death, yours to command."

Slowly, teasingly, he pulled his T-shirt up over his head, keeping eye contact until the last second. He tossed the shirt aside, closed his eyes and tilted his chin up. He said in a whisper, "My life is in your hands."

It was such a phony move, exactly like the old Adrian, that I nearly walked out.

But I didn't. Without quite knowing why, I touched the tip of the dagger to the hollow of his throat, where his pulse beat just below the surface of his skin. I gently traced the blade down his chest.

He was right. There *was* something seductive about it. I liked it. Liked it very much, in fact. Him open and vulnerable, and me with a dagger in my hand.

He shuddered and opened his eyes. His pupils were so dilated that his irises showed as thin blue rings. He took the dagger from me, sheathed it, set it aside. His breathing, fast and ragged, matched my own. He leaned toward me, but I shifted away, moving to the other side of the room.

He followed, stood close but not touching. I felt his breath, warm on my neck. From upstairs, I heard the faint ticking of a kitchen clock, marking the seconds.

"Help me light the candles," he said.

Adrian

I've set candles all around the room—soft white and inky black. We move in opposite directions, lighting them. My senses are amplified by The Power. I strike a match. The sulfur is a harsh burn in my nostrils. The flare of light is a shooting star across my retina. The hiss of wax catching fire is a windstorm in my ears.

"I don't know how to do this," she says.

"Trust me." I turn off the room lights, and put on my special make-out music. *Unchained Melody*. She's standing in front of the mirror on my wardrobe door. I slip my arms around her waist. "You're so beautiful."

"I'm fat," she says, blurting out the words before she can censor them.

"You are *not* fat."

She snorts. "Right. I'm not thin."

"So?" I kiss the back of her neck. "Why do girls always think guys like them anorexic? I like my women with some—"

"Meat on their bones?" she supplies, her voice acid.

"Curves," I say, pulling her even closer. "Soft, sweet, sexy curves."

She melts against me. We sway to the music. Warmth floods my body. Cold fire burns through my veins.

"Your eyes are glowing," she says. *Electric blue.*

"So are yours." *Red-gold, like a rising sun.*

Light plays around her, white and shimmering silver. In the mirror, I see my own aura, blue, flaring neon bright.

"The Power," I say. "The more I'm with you, the stronger it grows."

"I'm afraid," she says.

"Don't be." Our auras blaze, crackling with energy. "It's meant to be. It's why my father brought me here."

"Meant to be?"

"Us. Together. Like this." I run my hand down her arm. Sparks fly off from where I touch her, and she jerks, expecting pain. But the sparks only bring a kind of effervescence, like champagne bubbles bursting over her skin.

"It's part of the plan. Once we join, we'll be invincible."

"What are you saying?" she asks.

I'm so buzzed by The Power, I don't hear the warning in her voice.

"I want it so much, Gwen," I say.

She pulls away. Her aura dies. The temperature in the

room drops ten degrees. I don't understand. What did I say wrong?

Gwen

His words numbed me. *I want it so much, Gwen.*

I want *it* so much.

The Power.

I should have known. It was too good to be true.

A memory came to me. I was twelve, driving my first snowmachine. I'd crashed through thin ice near the shore. My father pulled me out, but I remember the shock of the frigid water, deadening me.

Like now.

"You don't want me," I said.

"What do you mean? I've never wanted anything more in my life."

He seemed confused. I nearly fell for it, but then *Unchained Melody* ended. A new song started. *When a Man Loves a Woman.* I punched the power button on his stereo. The music died. Walking around the room, I blew out the candles. I reached for the switch on the wall, bathing us in artificial light.

"Gwen?" He had the nerve to look bewildered.

"And to think I nearly fell for it. When a man loves a woman? This isn't love. This isn't even lust. Unless lusting for power counts."

"What are you talking about?"

"This!" I waved my hand around his room. "This whole

seduction scene. How gullible do you think I am?" He turned away, took several deep breaths, and loosened his hunched shoulders. When he turned back to me, he was composed, with a relaxed smile lifting the corners of his lips. He moved in close and locked eyes with me. A faint glow still played in their depths.

"I'm sorry," he said, dropping his voice. "I didn't mean it that way. Forgive me?"

For a second time, I fell under his spell. My body swayed toward his and the energy field around us sprang back to life. I wanted him to hold me, the way he'd held me in my dream. I wanted to see his face, open and vulnerable, the barrier down.

He smiled, ran a finger along the line of my jaw, tilted my chin up for a kiss. I looked deep into his eyes.

There was no love there. Only triumph.

"I nearly fell for it," I sputtered. "I should have trusted my instincts. Your kind can't be trusted."

Adrian

"Your *kind?*" I don't understand. What's going on here?

She walks around the room, waving her arms as if she's half-crazy. "You don't care about anyone but yourself. Everything is you, you, you. What can I get out of this? How will this make me look? What's in it for me?"

What? Where is she getting this from? What about *her?*

"You hypocrite. What did *you* get out of this, Gwen?" I see her thoughts. Her story about Mr. Dean, complete with a photo layout. Her new status at school; the status I gave her.

"Don't twist this around," she spits at me. "If I didn't share this Power thing of yours, you'd never have given me the time of day."

"Power *thing?*"

"Let me ask you a question," she says. "If you could have me, but had to give up The Power, would you?"

She flattens me with those words. Would I?

"That's what I thought." She yanks open my bedroom door, stomps into the family room. She grabs her snowmobile suit, hops around getting one leg in, then the other.

"Gwen, wait, please, give me a chance to explain," I say.

"You've got one minute," she says, sitting down on the couch.

The look in her eyes warns me not to sit next to her. I go over to the wood stove, throw in a log. Sparks fly up the flue.

Think!

"Clock's ticking," she warns.

I'm picking up her emotions—anger and hurt. I should say it's *her* I want, not The Power. But is it? How do you separate the two?

"Time's up." She gets up, heads for the door.

I grab her arm; pull her back down on the couch.

"Just listen for a second," I say.

"Let me go!" She tries to wriggle out of my grasp.

"No. Not until you listen."

She explodes. She's punching me. Trying to kick me. She lands a good one and I lose it. I pin her down. She struggles, but I'm stronger. She can't move.

That's when her eyes go wide with fear. I read her mind.

"*No*," I say. "It's not like that. I just want you to *listen*."

She doesn't believe me. She makes a noise, almost a growl. She imagines a cauldron of boiling oil, imagines tipping it over me, searing my skin, bubbling away layers and layers of—

I pull away, rubbing my arms. She has one *hell* of an imagination. For one moment, I'd felt my skin peel away, burned and blackened, leaving bloody red muscle underneath.

"That *hurt!*"

"Don't. Touch. Me. Ever. Again."

I back away. "Look . . . I'm sorry . . . I didn't mean to . . . I just . . . "

Wait. What did he mean? That hurt? How could he feel that unless he's reading my mind. He's been lying all along. That bastard!

"You bastard," she says. "You lied to me. You've been reading my mind all along."

She'll never speak to me again. I'm about to lose her. I'm desperate.

"I couldn't tell you. You'd have freaked. I had to lie. At least until I could gain your trust." I realize, too late, that I should have left out the trust part.

"Trust. You call this gaining my trust?" she yells. "So tell me, what else did you lie about?"

"Nothing. I swear."

Gwen

He was lying. I could tell by his body language. What happened next wasn't totally under my control. It was as if all the rage and hurt exploded from me. A ball of sizzling, snapping energy flew through the air, caught him square in the chest. He fell to the floor, struggling to catch his breath.

I finished getting into my snowmachine suit, jammed my feet into my boots, grabbed my helmet and gloves. I yanked open the sliding glass door. Frigid air rushed in.

I won't beg you to come back." His voice was whisper-soft, but it made the hair stand up on my neck.

"I shouldn't have come in the first place." I walked out into the darkness of the winter night.

Adrian

How had she done that? It felt as if someone whacked my chest with a sledgehammer. I'm flattened on the floor, shivering in the rush of bitter air. Getting up is not an option. Breathing even less so.

How could she attack me like that? She'd turned everything around. Simply because I'd said, "I want *it* so bad," not "I want *you* so bad." It was a slip of the tongue. And she was all over me for it. As if she'd judged me ages ago and was waiting for an excuse to hang me.

And that look in her eyes, when I pinned her down on the couch. That hurt. How could she even *think* that?

Gwen

The sky had clouded over, but there was enough diffused light reflecting off the snow to guide me home.

I shook with the effects of adrenaline rush. I'd been so right about him. He'd do anything to get what he wanted.

He'd think twice next time. I don't know how I'd thrown that ball of energy at him, but it had felt good. I would never let him get the upper hand again.

What had I been thinking? That he liked me? Wanted me? How naive could I be? I'd let him play me. *Use* me.

I should have trusted my instincts. I'd known who he was the moment I'd set eyes on him. But I'd liked the way he'd looked at me. Liked the hunger he'd awakened in me. The way the visions came to me when he was near. And to be honest, I'd enjoyed having something, for once, that Joanne didn't have.

But he'd been reading my mind all along! My private thoughts! What had he seen? I felt dirty. Exposed. He'd been in my *mind*. He'd taken away my freedom. I'd never forgive him for that.

I dragged myself up the path to our back door.

"Hi, Gwen," Mom called as I walked past the living room. "How'd the studying go?"

"Great."

"I was about to watch a movie. Want to join me?" she asked.

"Um, no, thanks. I'm going to bed. Worn out from all that studying," I said.

As I washed my face, I caught my reflection in the mirror. Red hair, green eyes, red lipstick. I looked like Melissa. Why hadn't I noticed that before? I'd changed for him. For his approval. As much as he'd betrayed me, I'd betrayed myself.

I grabbed my coat. "Mom, I'm heading into town."

"Goodness, what do you need at this hour?" asked Mom.

"Hair dye," I said. "And new glasses."

SUNDAY, JANUARY 26

Adrian

In the morning, I call Melissa.

"Hey, Handsome," she says. "How's it going?"

"Great," I answer. "Are you free tonight? Pizza and a movie?"

"What about *Gwennie*?"

The way she says *Gwennie* bugs me, but then I think, what's Gwen to me now?

"We were never really together," I say. "So, I'll pick you up at six?"

"Okay. Let me give you directions." She doesn't ask which show we'll see. There's only one movie theater in town. Only one show.

I spend a boring day at the funeral home, listening for the phone, cleaning, sweeping a light dusting of snow off the steps. My parents call once from Winnipeg, to check in. I tell them it's been quiet. No new clients. Just me, alone with my thoughts.

Every time I think about Gwen, I want to smash my fist through a wall. So I don't think about her.

I drive home, put whitening strips on my teeth, shower, shave, slap on pit juice and cologne, rinse my contacts and put them back in, remember to remove the whitening strips, and then brush, floss, and gargle. I dress in black jeans and a black sweater, and head back to town.

As soon as I pull up at Melissa's house, she's out the door, down the drive, and in my car.

"You look great," I tell her.

"Thanks. You, too." *Did I put my diaphragm in my purse?*

I hide my smile as she checks her purse. She remembered.

At the restaurant, we barely talk. She's mostly thinking about how good we look together. I'm mostly thinking about getting laid.

She visits the restroom while I pay the bill. I happen to glance over into a booth and see Jo and Conrad sitting together. What? They'd broken up, so what was he doing with her? I want to go over and ask. Maybe pound him in the face while I'm asking. But Melissa returns, links her arm through mine, and the opportunity passes.

When we get to the theater, I ask Melissa where she'd prefer to sit.

"Anywhere," she says.

I touch her thoughts. She likes the back row, in the double seat. The make-out seat. Fine with me. We get comfortable, my arm around her, her head resting on my shoulder. With my free hand, I stroke her hair. She makes a contented humming sound and rests her hand on my leg.

I'm suddenly struck with the weirdest craving. I want an anchovy pizza. What? I hate anchovies.

Click.

Gwen. She loves anchovy pizza. Double anchovies. Her craving, not mine. She's picking up the phone. Ordering a large.

I disconnect from her mind and put up a block. Only it doesn't work. I still want anchovy pizza. I can't escape. She's in me, deep inside my mind. I can't shake her.

I try to watch the movie. Melissa snuggles closer. I slide my hand down to brush against her breast. She murmurs, slides her hand farther up my thigh.

And then I break out laughing.

"Shhhh," warns a girl sitting two rows down.

I laugh harder. Melissa wonders if I've lost my mind. Maybe I have. I hold it in until I reach the men's room. Then I let loose.

Gwen's watching a funny movie. She's laughing so hard her abs ache. I lean against the wall, holding my gut, and laugh until tears stream down my face.

Some poor guy comes out of a stall, gives me a look of pure disgust as he races out. That sets me off again. It's a few more minutes before I get control. This isn't funny. What is she doing inside my head?

I return to my seat and Melissa. Dear, sweet, uncomplicated, wants-to-get-laid Melissa. The movie ends, and I realize I can't remember a single thing about the plot.

"Want to come back to my place?" I suggest.

"Sure."

We get into my car. I read her mind. She figures if I don't start things, she will. She imagines, in detail, exactly what she'll do.

I nearly drive off the road.

"You okay?" she asks.

"Yeah," I say, my voice kind of husky. I start a conversation about school, about the teachers, anything to distract her. It works. She spends the rest of the ride complaining about our English teacher. I do a lot of nodding and "uh huh-ing" and that satisfies her.

We arrive. I hang up her coat, show her around. We're in the kitchen.

"Would you like something? A Coke, maybe?" I ask.

"How about a drink?" she says.

"Uh, we don't have much selection, Melissa."

"Don't you drink?"

"All the time." My one experience was getting drunk with some guys from school back in Milwaukee. I hadn't liked the loss of control. Or the puking.

I open the pantry, hunt around. "How's this?" I ask, holding up a bottle of bourbon.

"It'll do."

I get her a glass. "Ice? Maybe Coke with it?"

"Straight."

I pour an ounce or so into the glass, set the bottle down. She chugs back the bourbon in one gulp, then half-fills the glass. Some splashes onto my mother's prized kitchen counter. I grab a paper towel and wipe it off.

"Where's your room?" Melissa asks.

We go downstairs, but I lead her to the couch in the family room instead. I throw a few logs into the woodstove. The fire crackles. Melissa's hair shines red in the firelight, reminding me for a moment of Gwen's eyes with The Power shining in them. I push away the memory and join Melissa on the couch.

Her drink is half gone. That bugs me. Does she have to drink to make out with me? But then her lips are on mine, and her tongue is in my mouth.

She tastes like bourbon, smooth and harsh and hot. She kisses me, hard, demanding. I pull off her top, reach around to undo the clasp of her bra.

"Wait," says Melissa. "Where's the bathroom?"

I point. She leaves, comes back a few minutes later. I know she's put in the diaphragm. I've set a selection of condoms on the coffee table. She checks them out, grabs a scented one.

We move into my bedroom.

"Oh, wow," she says, seeing the sword on my wall. She takes it down, starts to pull it out of its scabbard. I take it away from her.

"What's wrong?" she asks.

I don't know what's wrong. I just don't want her touching it.

"Come here." I sit on the bed. She climbs into my lap. I

run a finger along the curve of her neck and feel soft, soft skin. I lean in for a kiss.

"Oh, wait," she says. She reaches into her back pocket, brings out two pills. "Here."

"What are those?" I ask, but I can guess.

"They'll make you happy," she says.

"I'm already happy."

"Aw, c'mon Adrian. It's no big deal."

"No drugs."

She pops a pill into her mouth, swallows it down with the last of the bourbon. She takes the other pill, tries to force it between my clamped lips.

And it's *wrong*. The whole scenario. There's no energy. No aura. Nothing. And much as I am desperate to get laid, I'm not *that* desperate.

I stand, dumping her to the carpet. She stares up at me with a mix of surprise and anger.

"Get dressed," I tell her. "I'm taking you home."

Gwen

The ringing of a phone woke me up.

"Hey, cuz. Wanna go for breakfast?"

"Not hungry," I said, hanging up.

A few seconds later, the phone rang again.

"I'll be right there," Joanne said.

"No." Slam.

Ring. "Why are you so grumpy?"

"Why are you so obscenely cheerful?" I rubbed sleep out of my eyes and yawned.

"You know how Conrad kept calling me? Wanted to get back together? Well, I met him for pizza last night. I told him it's really, really over."

"Yeah?"

"Yeah. So then he went into his I-can't-live-without-you-Joanne routine. So I told him he'd have to because I won't go out with a guy who tells me who I can and who I can't talk to."

"Uh, huh," I obliged her by saying.

"And I told him I didn't like the way he never talks about his feelings. Never opens up to me. So then he said he loved me."

"He did?"

"Yeah. But I think he said that to get me back. So I walked out. I didn't even wait for the pizza. I simply walked out. Cool, huh?"

"Cool," I agreed. But there was something in her voice. It sounded too cheerful. Too forced.

"Yeah. So what's done is done, right?" Her voice shook on *right?*

I groaned. "Joanne? Why don't you call him? Give him another chance?"

"No way. He had lots of chances. Anyway, guess who I saw with Melissa?" She waited for me to respond. When I didn't, she said, "Adrian."

"I'm sure they'll be very happy together." My voice sounded bitter, even to myself.

"Want to tell me what happened?" Joanne asked.

"No."

"Okay. I'll be over in ten," she said.

I pulled the covers over my head. Exactly ten minutes later, Joanne yanked them off.

"Whoa, your hair! When did you dye it back?"

"Last night."

"I like it," Joanne said. "I didn't want to hurt your feelings, but I didn't think the red looked so good on you."

"*Now* you tell me?"

She scrunched up her face. "I'm sorry."

"It's okay. Just go away and let me sleep."

I burrowed back into the covers. Joanne grabbed my arm and pulled. I fell to the floor with a loud *thunk*.

A bulldog, my cousin.

"Okay, you win," I said, laughing. "Give me time to shower."

I dressed in my baggy jeans and an old sweatshirt. I checked myself out in the mirror. The sweatshirt had a big mustard stain on the front. I looked like the poster child for low self-esteem.

I rummaged in my closet. I found my new jeans and pulled them on. Considered one of my new tops. Melissa-type tops, with low-cut necklines, short enough to show my midriff.

Forget that. I found a turtleneck, a creamy white knit. It fit snugly, showing off my best feature. Features.

"Wow!" said Joanne as I came downstairs. "You look hot. Hey, are those new glasses?"

"Yup. Went to the one-hour place at the mall last night. They're some new kind of plastic. Lighter and thinner than my old ones."

"What was wrong with the contacts?" Joanne asked.

"They weren't me," I said, shrugging.

I filled Joanne in as she drove us into town.

"Like wait," Joanne said, turning to look at me. "You mean his eyes glowed? Like *glowed* glowed?"

"Yeah. Eyes on the road, Joanne," I warned her. "His eyes, his whole body."

I told her more, interspersing my story with the occasional, "eyes on the road, Joanne" and "hands on the wheel." Joanne interrupted a dozen times to clarify a point or push for more details. We arrived at the Burger Barn in time for me to tell her the last part.

"You poured boiling oil over him?" Joanne asked, getting out of the car.

"No. I *imagined it*. He was reading my mind, Joanne. He lied to me all along. It was his own fault."

"Yeah, but boiling oil? Isn't that a bit extreme?" Joanne led the way into the Barn, ordered two Western omelet bagel breakfasts. We found a table at the back, one of the roughhewn oak tables the Barn was famous for, and sat down opposite each other on the wooden benches.

"So, then what happened?" she prompted.

I continued the story. About him grabbing me, throwing me down on the couch.

Joanne mashed a hash brown into her mouth. A small piece stuck to her lip. I reached across and brushed it off.

"So, you socked him with a fireball?" she asked.

"I guess. Some kind of energy ball," I said.

"Whoa. Did you hurt him?"

"I don't know. Sort of. Maybe. He deserved it, Joanne. The whole thing was a setup. The music, the candles. Everything. He brought me there for one purpose."

"To make love to you," Joanne said.

"To screw me," I argued. "He thought having sex with me would increase his powers. He's a psychic vampire. He's been using me."

"Really? I thought it went both ways."

"What?"

"Your power has grown, too. First the dreams, now the visions. It's mutual."

"Mutual? If it's so mutual, why did he prevent me from leaving? Why did he pin me down?"

"You were attacking him. He was protecting himself."

"Why are you taking his side? Because you dumped Conrad? Is that it? Do you want Adrian? Well, you can have him."

"It'd serve you right if I did go after him!" Joanne exploded.

"It's what you've wanted all along," I said.

"No. What I wanted, all along, was for you to be happy. But, oh, no, not you. What are you afraid of? Letting someone into that fortress you've built around yourself?"

"That's better than you," I retorted. "A new boyfriend every month. You're as bad as Melissa."

Joanne's mouth dropped open. "How can you *say* that? I've never slept with any of them. It's called *dating*. That's what you're supposed to do in high school, Gwen. *Date*. You know, like go out, have fun?" Her voice faltered and her eyes filled with tears.

"I'm sorry, Joanne," I said. "I didn't mean it. It was a stupid thing to say."

Her tears overflowed, landed in wet splotches on her half-eaten bagel. I dabbed at her face with a napkin.

"Look," I said, "ever since Stone—"

"Gwen," Joanne interrupted. She sounded worn out. "Let it go already. He apologized. He even asked you out. And you turned him down."

"I don't accept charity," I said, bristling.

"What do you mean? Charity?"

"You think I didn't find out? About you paying him? Twenty bucks to take out your loser cousin? How do you think that made me feel?"

"Paid him? Are you nuts? Who told you that?"

"Melissa."

"And you believed *her*?" Joanne asked quietly. "You didn't even come to me? You didn't ask me if it was true?"

"Oh, Joanne . . . " She was right. I should have asked her. Should have trusted her. "I'm sorry."

"It's okay. Water under the bridge. Uh, you finished eating?"

I'd only left a small bite of bagel. "I'm done. You going to finish yours?"

"Nah. I'm not hungry." She threw away the rest of her breakfast and headed out of the restaurant.

I followed. "Joanne? I really am sorry."

"Don't worry about it," she said. "I'm not mad at you."

But she wasn't smiling, either. And when she came to a frozen chunk of snow in the middle of the path, she gave it a vicious kick, sending snow chunks flying in all directions.

MONDAY, JANUARY 27

Adrian

I'm sitting in English, surviving the icy blast of emotion that Gwen throws my way. She's wearing a suede skirt, boots, and a brown turtleneck that matches her hair. She looks classy, like a sexy eyeglasses model. She catches me staring. She thinks, very clearly, *you could have had me, but you blew it.* Then she shuts me out of her mind. Recites the alphabet in French. Conjugates verbs, also in French. Sings *Frère Jacques*, every last verse.

Her stomach contracts with hunger. She had skipped

breakfast. She's punishing me. She remembers how I reacted the day she was suffering cramps from her period. *Probably something I ate,* I'd said. She's put two and two together. Knows I was reading her mind. Figures if she's hungry, there's a good chance I'll be hungry, too.

She's sneaky and she's smart. I have to admire that.

Meanwhile, her hunger gnaws at me. It's like the guilt that gnaws at me, telling me something I don't want to hear. Don't want to think about.

English ends and I go to my other classes. When I'm not in the same room, the hunger lessens. But, it's still there, like a burr in my brain.

Lunchtime arrives. I look around for a table. Can't sit with Gwen. Can't sit with Melissa. I find an open table near the entrance to the cafeteria. I watch Gwen nibble on a bowl of plain lettuce. I wolf down a tuna on rye, a protein bar, and an apple.

And I'm still hungry.

Jo walks by.

"Hey, Jo!" I say. "Have a seat."

She glances over at Gwen, but sits down. I catch Gwen's thoughts. *Fine. Take him. See if I care.*

So I was right. Jo likes me. Good. Time to go for what I wanted from the beginning.

Except Jo isn't looking her usual friendly self. "How was your date with Melissa?" *Don't waste much time, do you?*

I pour on the old charm, tilt my head, and smile. "You could have warned me."

"Could have warned you? That Melissa's the school bicycle?"

"The what?"

"Everyone gets a turn." Joanne says, quite serious. "So did you?" *Take a ride?*

I lean toward her, close but not touching. Drop my voice into the seduction range like I've practiced. "Now, that would be telling, wouldn't it?"

Get real, she thinks. *Drop the act.*

That sets me back. She's not buying it. Not for a second. I try changing the subject. "So, how was your date with Conrad?"

"I told him it's over," she says.

"So you're free to go out with me tonight."

Jo gives a mental laugh. *You think you can have me that easy? Bomb out with Gwen, try to jump Melissa, then hit on me?*

I try one last time. "C'mon, Jo. You like me. I like you. What's the problem?"

"Gwen. She's my cousin." Jo shoves a forkful of fries into her mouth. A blob of gravy drips on her chin, but she doesn't notice.

"Is it because of some story she told you about Friday night?" I tap into Jo's mind, see images, bits of conversation. All damning. "Did she say I tried to force her to have sex with me? Is that what she said?"

"So did you?" *Try to force her?*

"No!" I slam my hand down on the table. Jo's milkshake quivers. "If she said that, she's a lying b—"

"*Hey!* Watch your mouth." I've never seen Jo mad before, but I'm seeing it now. What is it with these two? They're like she-lions, the way they protect each other.

I take a deep breath. I catch myself tapping my fingers. Stop. Then I give Jo my best little-boy smile. "Yes, ma'am."

"Drop the act," she snaps.

"Jo, what do you expect me to do? Go crawling back to her? Beg forgiveness? I didn't do anything wrong."

"You *hurt* her." Jo gives me this level look, like she's not backing down.

"The hurt went both ways, Jo," I say, getting up to leave. "By the way, there's gravy on your chin."

Gwen

I should have trusted Joanne. But when she sat down with Adrian, it was as if she'd put rat poison in my salad. I couldn't hear what they were saying, but Adrian's body language was obvious. He was moving in on her. No surprises there.

My heart ached to remember Friday night and his arms around me. I'd lost him.

Ha! Who was I kidding? I'd never actually had him. The truth was he'd never desired me. I wasn't a love interest. Not even a sex object. I was more of an electrical outlet. He wanted to plug in and recharge.

But I *missed* him. Not just the attention, or the flowers or the compliments. I missed talking, about music and books and movies. We'd started to open up to each other, to get to know each other.

What if there had been no Power? What if he and I had come together without it? I could imagine being with him. Maybe watching a movie and eating popcorn. Or sitting in front of the woodstove, drinking hot chocolate and talking.

Good one. Without The Power, he'd never have noticed me. My kind and his kind don't mix.

I looked over to see Adrian slam his hand down on the table. They're arguing? Adrian glanced at me. They're arguing about me? He got up, stalked away.

Joanne was defending me?

I left for the newspaper, feeling ashamed for doubting my own cousin.

Doug was on the phone when I arrived. He handed me my assignment without skipping a beat. I gave him a thumbs-up and left.

I read it over in the car. *Great*. Cover the grand opening of a new gas station. I'd hoped, after Mr. Dean's story, that Doug might give me something more challenging. I'd never get that summer internship with stupid assignments like this.

The grand opening of the gas station was a grand bore. There were balloons and banners and free coffee and doughnuts. Now, there's front page news.

I did a short interview with the gas station manager, took a few photos, and wrote down the impressions of a few customers. "Nice clean bathrooms," said one woman. "Twenty-four-hour convenience," said her husband.

Yup, I'd probably win an award with this one. What I needed was a story. What I needed was another vision.

TUESDAY, JANUARY 28

Adrian

There's a stone ledge that separates the hallway from the sunken cafeteria. I sit there, watching the action below. Two girls, probably freshmen, sit together at the other end of the ledge. They smile at me, whisper, giggle. Yeah, you wish, I think. I'm not *that* desperate.

Gwen reads a book. *War and Peace.* I touch her mind, but all I get is the image of a stone castle, high on a cliff, drawbridge pulled up. She looks up at me and gives me a small satisfied smile. She's skipped breakfast again. She's having a diet soda for lunch. And I'm starving, like a beggar at a banquet.

No. Like an addict craving his next fix.

I cast my mind around the room. Distraction, that's what I need. The strongest emotions catch my attention first. Like that girl over there, talking to her friend. Her grandmother is in the hospital. Might not live. I block her thoughts. I don't need to feel her pain. My father's an idiot for not learning how to tune that out of his life.

There's a guy halfway across the cafeteria. I don't know his name. He's almost pissing his pants with anxiety. Curious, I probe deeper. I see he's the one supplying half the school with happy drugs, as Melissa calls them. Carrying a thousand bucks in the back pocket of his jeans. No wonder he's nervous.

For one second, I'm tempted. I could wait for him after school. Call him out. Demand the money. It's drug money. He doesn't have the right to keep it. Yeah, right, and the next day I'd find six or seven of his friends waiting to beat me up. Not a great idea.

I'm so hungry. And I want a smoke. Well, why not? Just one pack. Take the edge off the hunger. I head to town, and go into a variety store. The guy at the register looks like a high school dropout.

"You legal?" He scratches at a zit on his face. It starts to bleed.

"Yes," I lie.

"Need to see some ID," he says, grabbing a tissue and pressing it to his face.

"Left it at home."

"Can't sell you nothin' then."

I stare into his eyes. I draw on The Power, drop my voice down, slow and even. "I won't tell and you won't tell. Anyone asks, you checked my card."

"Yeah," he says, looking bored. "Whatever."

He hands over the package. I smoke one before getting in my car. The buzz hits me in seconds. Guess that's what a year of abstinence does to you. I'm still feeling the nicotine rush when I return to school and go to Psychology. We're no more than ten minutes into the class before Gwen has a vision.

A van will crash through the ice. McCallum Point. Because he turns off the ice road. Thinks the ice is safe.

Ice road?

Gwen looks over at me. *Well?*

Well, what? I pass her a piece of paper. NOT MY PROBLEM.

Fine, she thinks at me. *I'll go myself.*

As soon as she thinks that, she gets a new vision.

It's her, running out, trying to warn the van. The ice cracks. The van sinks, taking Gwen with it.

My hand shakes as I write another note. YOU WIN.

She looks as smug as Cleo bringing a dead bird to the door.

"Ahem." That's Mrs. Janzen, our teacher.

"May I see you outside, please?" She's Canadian-polite but ice-cube cold. We follow her into the hallway.

"You know the rules in my classroom," Mrs. Janzen says. "Flirt on your own time."

Gwen opens her mouth to argue, closes it when she sees the expression on Mrs. Janzen's face.

"I'm knocking your participation grades to zero," she continues.

Gwen's mental expression of dismay hits me hard. She actually *cares* about participation points. So, I move in close to Mrs. Janzen, look into her eyes, pitch my voice hypnotically low. I draw on The Power. "Mrs. Janzen, you don't want to do that."

"I beg your pardon?"

"You don't want to do that," I repeat, using *the voice*. "Gwen is your best student. She didn't disrupt the class."

"Perhaps *disrupt* is the wrong term, but—"

"Gwen is your best student," I repeat. I hold her in my gaze. Don't let her look away. Beside me, Gwen gasps. I motion for her to be still.

Mrs. Janzen looks uncertain. "Yes, of course, but—"

"Gwen and I are leaving now. You'll inform the attendance office that we're officially excused."

"Of course. Officially excused. Go on, then." She waves us away, returns to the classroom.

"How did you do that?" Gwen asks with a mix of awe and fear.

"Does it matter? Are you coming or not?"

She thinks about the pictures she will take. About the headline in the paper.

"I feel like I'm making a pact with the Devil," she says.

Gwen

We met in the parking lot.

"I'll follow you," he said.

We drove past the Burger Barn, down to the lake. I pulled out onto the ice road and heard the beep of a car horn behind me. I looked in the rearview mirror. He pointed.

Ice road, I sent to him.

He raised his hands in an exaggerated shrug.

Once the ice freezes deep enough to hold a car, you clear a road through the snow, I sent. *The lack of snow cover causes the ice road to freeze even deeper. It's totally safe as long as you don't go off the road.*

He shook his head, as if I were crazy.

Just keep your window open. For a quick escape.

Adrian

This is seriously weird. I'm on the surface of a frozen lake, following a plowed road marked only by small evergreens stuck into the snow on either side. I crank down my window, turn off my radio, and listen for cracking ice. We drive maybe three miles. Gwen pulls over. I park behind her. Ahead is a large building. A sign says *McCallum Lodge*.

Gwen, camera ready, walks a short distance along the ice.

"Gwen, wait." I catch up to her. "Listen, we can save him."

"Duh. Isn't that why we're here?"

"No, I mean, we can stop it from happening." And I won't have to crawl out on the ice to rescue the guy, I'm thinking.

"I saw him going through, Adrian. It's meant to happen."

I shut up. I'm thinking she sees the future she wants to see.

I hear the rumble of a vehicle. A rusty old van appears from around a bend in the ice road. I flag it down. The driver stops. He's another old guy, like Mr. Dean. His liver-spotted hands grip the wheel.

"Hey, son. What's up?" he asks.

"You can't go that way, sir," I tell him, pointing off the road. "There's current there. Ice is too thin."

"Nah, the ice is fine. I've lived here all my life, son. My fishing buddy, Jake, lives out that way. Been there hundreds of times."

"This winter is different. The conditions—"

He interrupts. "Look, son, I know you mean well, but I've got to be on my way now."

So I use *the voice*. "You will go back to town. Call Jake and tell him you're not coming."

He backs up. Good, he's going to turn around and leave. Then he guns the engine, roars past me.

What?

He drives about thirty feet before the ice breaks. It's like watching an instant replay. The back end of the van disappears first. The man scrambles out of the window, grabs onto the edge of ice.

I feel his panic. I run toward him, scared out of my mind. They don't teach ice rescues where I come from.

Gwen has a vision. I see myself falling through the ice. *Whoa.* I stop. Her vision changes. I'm going to crawl. Okay, then. I drop to my belly, and commando-crawl.

The man flails around. He tries to grip the ice, slides back into black water.

Why am I doing this? I'm nuts. The ice creaks beneath me. Freezing water flows over the edge, creeps closer, as if to pull me in.

I see the shifting visions in Gwen's mind, each one a possible outcome. I'll make it, as long as I don't chicken out. If I lose my nerve, get to my feet too soon, the ice will give way beneath me. Okay, no chickening out, then.

I wiggle out of my coat and slide it along the ice, guided by Gwen's visions. The man grabs the arm of my coat, loses his grip, grabs again. I inch backward, pulling him out. It takes forever. Probably only a few seconds, but it takes forever.

Finally, we're far enough away from the hole that I relax. That's when I hear sirens. When did she call?

The ambulance guys take care of the man. Mr. Fogerty. They try to talk me into coming back to the hospital, but I insist I'm okay. All I need is to get into my car and turn the heat up.

"I'm going to the hospital to follow up," Gwen says.

I sense something in her mind. Something cold and calculating.

"You manipulated me," I say, realizing the truth. "You used me to get your story."

"So? The shoe is on the other foot. How does it fit, Adrian?"

My muscles go tight; my hands form fists. I fight for control. The worst thing is that I'd save the old guy again in a heartbeat. Risk my life all over again, just to be near her. To feel The Power run through her. To feel it run through me.

She drives off. Hands shaking, I light up a cigarette and inhale deeply. One more addiction hardly matters.

WEDNESDAY, JANUARY 29

Gwen

He was right. I'd manipulated him. I'd discovered something about the visions. I could pull them to me, could see multiple outcomes. Maybe it was because of that night at his house. So close, touching, the energy surging between us. So now the visions came more easily. I'd had a bad moment when the ice cracked under him. But the vision had shown him getting out safely. I had to trust that.

In the end, we both got what we wanted. He had his

picture on the front page of the paper. It was a beautiful shot. Crisp, clear, more real than life itself.

The headline was wrong, though. I'd submitted the story as, "Dramatic Rescue Saves Man's Life." But Doug had changed it. "Man in Coma After Dramatic Rescue."

I asked Doug about it when I went into the office.

"Yeah, poor old guy," Doug said. "He had a heart attack late last night. Probably the water was too much of a shock for him, eh?"

I nodded, feeling numb.

"That reminds me. Have you seen the police reports today? Bad news about that guy, the one who outran the train."

He handed over the police report.

A Rocky Waters resident, identified as Mr. James Dean, was killed in a single car accident late Friday night. It is suspected that Mr. Dean may have fallen asleep at the wheel. Alcohol is not considered to be a factor in his death.

"Too bad," said Doug. "I guess his time was up."

Adrian

The rescue story appears the next day in the paper. People at school congratulate me. Clap me on the back. I'm a local hero. Even if the poor old guy is in a coma, the fact remains that I saved his life.

At lunchtime, Jo catches me at the door to the cafeteria.

She's holding a stack of notebooks. I expect she'll congratulate me like everyone else, but she has other things on her mind.

"Hey, Adrian. Guess what? I'm back with Conrad," she says. "He came over last night. Look at this."

She hands me a notebook. It's filled with sketches. Jo leaning over to whisper a secret into Gwen's ear. Jo at debate practice, intensity in her face. Jo asleep in class, her head on the desk, a thin line of drool dribbling from her mouth.

That line of drool tells me everything.

"He's an *artist,* Adrian," Jo says, like it's a good thing. "He didn't want anyone to know. Isn't that dumb? He said the guys on the hockey team might think he was gay."

"Is he?" I ask, hoping.

She smiles. "No. He's loved me since JK. Isn't that sweet?"

"Yeah. Sweet."

"You and I can still be friends, right?"

"Yeah. Friends."

Then Jo looks past me and waves to someone. I turn around. It's Conrad.

"Hey, man," he says. He slides an arm around Jo's waist.

Sure. Rub my nose in it.

"C'mon. Let's all sit together," Jo suggests.

I look around the cafeteria. Melissa is sitting with Stone. Huh? I guess they're back together. Hard to keep track these days.

Jo is still waiting. "Okay," I say, accepting her offer. It's better than sitting alone. But then Jo waltzes over and sits at Gwen's table. Imagine my joy. Gwen has her face in a book. *Crime and Punishment.* In front of her sits a plastic container filled with lettuce. She ignores it.

My stomach growls in unison with hers. What is this anyway? Hungry when she's hungry? What did I do to deserve this?

I open my container of homemade chicken salad. Before Gwen can protest, I grab her lettuce and dump half my chicken salad on the side of it. She shoots me an evil look.

"Eat it before I shove it down your throat." I'm so hungry I nearly snarl.

"Poor boy. Hungry?"

"You *know* I am."

"Beg me."

"*What?*"

"Beg."

"Fine. Gwen, I'm begging you. Eat it before I shove it down your throat."

She giggles. She's *enjoying* this! "Okay," she says, taking a huge bite of chicken salad. "Hmmm, not bad."

I want to strangle her. Conrad and Joanne exchange a look of *what's with them?* I don't bother to explain.

Conrad says, "I've noticed you drive an old Mustang." So we talk about that. Meanwhile, Gwen eats the chicken. My navel unsticks from my spine.

"Want to come over tonight for a game of hockey?" Conrad asks me. Suspicious of his motives, I check his thoughts. He's feeling guilty that he'd ordered Jo not to talk to me. Thinks he might score some points with Jo if he befriends me. Wants to satisfy her need to see us as one big, happy family. Feels sorry for me, moving around so much, not having any guy friends.

If there's anything I've learned, reading minds, it's that people's motives are never simple.

"So you interested?" Conrad prompts.

"I, uh, that is, I—"

"Don't tell me you don't know how to skate," Conrad says.

Right then, both Gwen and Joanne tune in. I feel like an idiot. These people probably skated before they could walk.

"No problem," Conrad grins. "I'll teach you. Even loan you a pair of skates."

"Uh, okay." He seems like an okay guy. Dumb jock, but otherwise okay. And let's face it, I could use a friend.

When I go home for dinner, Mom greets me with the newspaper in her hand. She gives me a big hug. Dad claps me on the shoulder, says, "Well done, son." But then Mom asks, "How did you happen to be there, Adrian?"

I see the suspicion in her mind. So I lie. I *have* to. There is no other choice.

"Uh, Gwen wanted to show me an ice road. We were there when the van showed up and went through the ice."

"Gwen?" Her mother's radar goes into overdrive. "She wrote that other article, too, didn't she? About the train. The first time you were in the paper?" And she's thinking of my words: *Mom, do you believe in ESP?*

"Yeah. I was in town getting paint. I guess it was coincidence that I drove past right then."

She doesn't believe me, but she has no evidence against me. Dad's a different story. He tunes in to my emotions. He knows I'm lying. He doesn't confront me, that's not his style. But he knows I'm lying.

Mom makes a cherry pie for dessert. It's my favorite, but it tastes flat and metallic in my mouth. I have to get out of here. Escape their questions; escape my guilt.

I head over to Conrad's after dinner. Two of his brothers are there, plus a couple of guys from school. Conrad laces me into skates and hands me a stick. He makes me the goalie, which suits me fine. Less skating. I listen to the guys' blades slice across the ice, feel the bite of acid air in my lungs, watch the Northern Lights flare green and white in the blue-black sky.

Finally, when my ankles ache from standing up and my butt hurts from falling down, I head home.

THURSDAY, JANUARY 30

Gwen

It was one of those houses that could be anywhere. One-story, white stucco.

It was a man who could be anyone. I couldn't see his face, only the back of him, as he walked around the building, checking doors, windows.

Then, I saw the house from the outside, blazing against a dark winter sky. Fire trucks, ambulance, police.

And Adrian. Standing there. Watching it burn.

Adrian

I wake up, before dawn, with choking smoke in my room.

Fire!

"Cleo!" I hunt frantically on the bed, find her, scoop her into my arms and race out of the room. Cleo gives a surprised and angry yowl in my ear, scratches my bare chest. I ignore her efforts to escape and race toward the stairs.

I come to my senses with one foot on the bottom step. I am buck-naked, holding one extremely pissed-off cat. There is no fire. Gwen is dreaming.

Cleo rakes me again and I let her go. She bounds away, leaping up the stairs two at a time. I am now fully awake and in a bad mood.

I work out for an hour, shower, and head upstairs to whip up breakfast. I hear the shower running in my parent's bedroom. I get out the stuff I need for a protein shake, but stop dead in my tracks. I'm picking up my father's thoughts. He's in the shower and he's not alone.

You filthy bastard. What is it with you and that shower? That's my mother!

Yeah, and that's her husband, I remind myself. Leave. Leave now. I drive to school, now in a *very* bad mood.

I pull into the parking lot. There's Melissa, talking to good old Stone. He's leaning back against his car, a new SUV. She's leaning into him, her hands on the front of his jacket. *Is everybody getting some but me?*

But as I lock my car door and start toward the school, I see all is not well with the happy couple. He pushes her away. Curious, I stay where I am. They're too wrapped up in each other to notice me. I'm too far away to hear them, but I can read the echo of their words in their minds.

Stone: *I can't believe you. We're back together a week and you screw someone else? How could you do this to me?*

Melissa: *We didn't do anything. I told you. We went out for a coffee.*

Stone: *Sure. At least three of my friends saw you with him. Your tongue was halfway down his throat.*

Melissa: *We kissed. That's all. Just kissed.*

Stone: *Do I look that stupid? I don't understand you, Melissa. I don't understand why I keep coming back to you. Is there anyone you haven't done?*

Melissa's face turns almost as red as her hair. She pulls back her hand and smacks him, hard, across the face. He raises his hand, and—

I'm there in a few steps. I grab Stone from behind and yank back with my arms, hauling him off his feet. Melissa bursts into tears, and runs into the school.

Stone struggles to break loose. I'm holding him a few inches off the ground. He's not that light, but I'm pumped.

"Wrong move, dude," I tell him. "I'd suggest you calm down."

He grunts as I force the air out of his lungs.

"I press two hundred," I inform him. "How about you?"

"Dunno," he wheezes. Some of the fight goes out of him. He's willing to rough up a girl half his size, but doesn't want to go up against me.

"Play nice?" I relax my grip enough to let him draw some air.

He gets the message. "Yeah."

I give him one more jerk with my arms, then release him. He checks me out, recognizes me, straightens his jacket, and walks away.

I'm suddenly in a much better mood.

Gwen

All day Friday, the vision pushed into my waking world. At school, sitting in the cafeteria, I smelled smoke. I saw flames licking up the walls, reaching for the ceiling. I blinked. There was no flame. Breathed in. No smoke.

Driving home, I heard sirens. Pulled over to let the fire truck go by. Waited. No fire truck, no sirens. No fire.

Except in my head. Flame, smoke, sirens. A man restrained by the police, struggling to break free. Yellow hoses, spurting jets of water, heat, noise, confusion. And Adrian.

I told my parents I felt ill, had a bath, and went to bed early. At ten-thirty, I woke up, gasping. Fire, flame, smoke. I sneaked downstairs. The lights were out, my parents already asleep.

I got in the car and drove to town.

Adrian

Fire, flame, smoke.

I jerk awake, almost falling out of my chair. Disoriented, I look around. I'm in a visitation room, sitting beside a coffin with a dead guy for company. I must have dozed off.

I find my father in the office, looking over the details of tomorrow's funeral. I tell him I'm done for the night. He assumes I'm going home. I don't bother to correct him. I race out the back way of the funeral home and hop in my car. A siren wails a few blocks away. I head toward the sound.

I arrive before Gwen. Flames rocket from the windows of the house. Black smoke billows into the sky. Firefighters move with methodical speed, wrestling a yellow fire hose, shouting above the crackle and roar of the fire. Police cars and ambulances stand waiting, their lights fragmenting the night.

Two firefighters exit the building. I read their minds. They couldn't reach the upper floor. The fire is too intense.

Gwen arrives. She sees me, wonders what I'm doing there. Wonders how I got there so fast.

That's it. I'm gone. There's nothing I can do, anyway. Then I hear a voice in my head.

I don't want to die.

Images hit me. Too fast, too hard, too strong. Huddled on the floor. Breathing in smoke. Choking. Flames racing up the wall.

Help me.

I try to block. I can't. I'm there with her, locked in her mind, on the floor of her bedroom, surrounded by smoke and flame. I stagger back.

Can't breathe. Smoke. Burning my lungs. Can't . . .

My knees fold. I sink to the ground, to the cold, cold snow but what I feel is—

Hot, hot, hot.

She's dying.

"I'm sorry. I'm so sorry." I'm not sure, but I think I say the words out loud.

I feel her spirit separate. I come back into myself. Look around. Noise. Heat. Water jetting from fire hoses. Shouting. A sickening *crack* as the roof collapses.

None of it matters. She's free now.

Another car. Another person. A man.

"Celina!" he screams. He rushes toward the burning house, but the police hold him back. He yells at them, "Let me go! My wife's in there!"

The police lead him to an ambulance. He slumps over, his face in his hands. He doesn't see what I see. A swirl of light, like tiny fireflies. It twirls and spins, then slows and comes to rest in front of him. She's pure energy, awesome.

He doesn't know she's there.

The apparition moves across the road, a vortex of sparks, stopping in front of me. I hear, clearly, a voice in my mind: *Tell him the pink heart is in the upper right-hand drawer. Tell him he was the first and only.*

Yes, I answer without speaking, without questioning. Her energy loses form, hangs in the air around me. I drink it in and grow strong.

Gwen stands a few feet away. I see myself through her eyes. I'm a living torch, brighter than the flames that consume the house. The Power spills out of me and pours into her. It sings in her blood.

She puts two and two together. Knows there was a person in the house. Knows she died. She looks at me in fear and revulsion.

It rips me apart.

128

Gwen

I'd felt it. The Power. A rush, a torrent, flowing into me.

The woman died. And Adrian's Power increased. It doesn't take a genius to figure out how.

Enough. Focus on the story. This one could land me that summer internship.

The newspaper office was empty. The only sound was the subdued tapping of my keyboard as I fed the story to the computer.

I've never been high—not drugs or alcohol or anything—but that night I was wired. A writer's high, I told myself. One of those times when the words spill out of their own accord. One of those times when you must write, because the story compels you to write. Only I knew it was more than that.

I was drunk on The Power.

I wrote until two in the morning, then drove home. The moon had set. The night sky splintered into a million shards of light. The stars rained down on me.

SATURDAY, FEBRUARY 1

Adrian

Cleo bats at my face to wake me. I swat at her instinctively, still spooked from last night. She's not happy with that. I rack up a few more scratches. Feral cat. Should get rid of her. But, hey, she was a stray. She has issues.

I cook up some eggs and check the paper. Gwen's story appears on the front page, complete with color photos. On the third page of the paper is her background story about arson. She takes up half the paper. And she accused me of abusing The Power?

Later in the day, my dad gets the call to arrange the funeral. Flowers arrive, one display after another. I arrange them around Celina's coffin. One memorial, a heavy ring of roses, falls over when my back is turned. I jump. *Celina? Are you here?* But I don't feel her in the room.

The husband, Carl, arrives in time for visiting hours. He feels like he's been hollowed out like a pumpkin, only someone's forgotten to put the candle inside.

Visitors come, say the same thing. So sorry for your loss. A tragedy. Hope they catch the guy who did this. Carl nods. Shakes hands. Hugs. Cries a bit, but not much. He's maybe forty, stocky, short hair.

The visitors go. Carl stays, kneeling at his wife's coffin, praying. I remember Celina, and the message she asked me to pass on.

"Carl," I say, "there's something you need to know."

He follows me, obedient as a child, into the coffee room. I pour him a cup of coffee, double cream, no sugar, and hand it over. He's too deep in his grief to wonder how I knew how to fix it.

"I saw your wife," I say. "After she died. She appeared to me."

His head jerks up. The dullness leaves his eyes.

"She was beautiful. Like a galaxy of tiny stars."

"You saw her?" says Carl. "I don't understand."

"I have a gift," I say.

He nods, half-believing.

"She gave me a message, to tell you the pink heart is in the upper right-hand drawer."

He buries his face in his hands.

The Valentine I gave her in kindergarten.

"She also said you were the first and only," I continue.

Her first love. Her only love.

"And she's waiting for you, on the other side." That part I make up, but I figure it's possible.

Carl loses it. Sobs like a baby. I touch his shoulder and share his grief.

My father is standing in the doorway. He heard everything. He's proud of me.

Even if I couldn't read his mind, I'd be able to see that.

SUNDAY, FEBRUARY 2

Gwen

I ran into town first thing to grab a dozen copies of the paper. My photographs were awesome, and my copy, in my opinion, was professional.

I hid the papers, not wanting to field questions from Mom. The rest of the day was quiet. I did homework, read *Crime and Punishment*, had dinner. But all I could think about was the fire. Adrian shining like a hot blue star. Did he feed on death? Was that it? Suck up that woman's soul? What lengths would he go to for The Power?

That night, a dream woke me up. I sat bolt upright in bed.

Adrian, crouching over a dead deer, The Power radiating from his eyes, his aura lighting up the night.

MONDAY, FEBRUARY 3

Adrian

Monday comes. I'm hopeful that the link forged in the fire will bring us together.

Yeah. Right.

She's subzero, reciting the alphabet in French in her head until I'm ready to throttle her. We sit together at lunch, Conrad, Joanne, and I, but she refuses to acknowledge me. I place food beside her, like some weird offering to a goddess. She accepts it, eats it—tuna fish on wheat bread, a protein bar, and milk.

I want to talk to her. Explain what happened at the fire. But she won't even look at me.

We're sitting there, Conrad and me talking cars, when a vision comes to her. She tries to suppress it, but my hand shoots out and touches her arm. I lock into her mind and live the vision with her.

Pink house, purple shutters. The address, 10 Talbott Street, is on the mailbox. The front door opens. A man hurries to his truck. The door remains ajar.

A small child walks out, waddles down the drive, waves good-bye as the truck drives away. Behind the child, the front door swings shut.

The toddler tries to reach the doorbell. He pounds the door with his puny fist. No one comes. The child slumps on the doorstep, sucking his fingers, crying softly.

Gwen emerges from the vision, shoots me a poisonous look. But it's too late. I've seen it. So at ten that night, when I feel her getting into her car, I get into mine.

I arrive to find the child huddled on the doorstep, his fingers and toes already numb. I pick him up, tuck him inside my coat, and ring the doorbell. Inside, a television blares. Right as I'm about to bust in, I sense a woman walking down the hall.

"But he was in bed," she exclaims, taking her son from me. I tell her I was walking by and noticed him. She thanks me, and whisks the little guy away.

And Gwen watches, and does nothing.

Gwen

There was nothing I could do. Even if I saved him, he'd die a few days later. Drown in the bathtub or get hit by a car. You can't cheat death. Ask Mr. Dean. Saved from a train to die in a car accident. Or Mr. Fogerty. I'd called the hospital to check on his progress. He'd slipped away, going from coma to death with a quiet blip on his heart monitor.

I'd tried to hide the vision from Adrian. Wasn't about to let him feed again. But he'd touched me. He'd seen. Big surprise when he showed up at the scene. Maybe hoping I wouldn't be there? Hoping he could wait around until the kid died. Well, of course he couldn't.

I was watching him.

So, he scooped up the kid and carried him into the house. A few moments later, he came out. I could tell how angry he was by the way he walked. He yanked open the door of my car.

"The camera," he ordered.

"No." Who did he think he was?

He reached into the backseat, grabbed the camera.

"Hey!"

He ignored me, and deleted my shots of the kid.

"What were you planning to do with the photos, Gwen?"

"Nothing."

"Then why did you take them?" He slammed the door so hard the whole car shook.

Adrian

Her moral values are seriously in question. That's what I'm thinking as I hit the sweeping curve on Eagle Lake Road. My back wheels skitter on the ice. I downshift, cut my speed. I'm nearly through the curve when—

Wham!

I've hit something. My car spins, slides toward the far ditch. Swearing, I counter-steer, bring it under control, pull to the side of the road.

My front grill is smashed. My hood is crumpled. What happened?

And then I feel it.

Pain, fear, confusion.

A deer. There's blood everywhere. I strip off my gloves, and place my hands on her side. I try to pour my own energy into her. She feels warmth spreading from my hands, moving through her, calming her.

But it's not enough. I know the exact second her life force departs. It hovers around her body, an indistinct pattern of glowing energy. It swirls around me, touches me.

I drink it in. It tastes like cool spring water in my mind.

That's when Gwen drives by. I see myself through her eyes—crouched in the snow beside the deer, my eyes glowing, my aura bright around me, lighting up the night.

TUESDAY, FEBRUARY 4

Gwen

He had the nerve to put a protein bar on my desk in the morning.

Get lost, I thought. *Starve, for all I care.*

He said nothing, but I saw by the color in his face that he'd heard me.

I couldn't keep my mind on English. All I could think of was Adrian, crouched in the snow, The Power burning through his eyes, his hands stained with blood. Had he deliberately killed the deer? To recharge his batteries? Or had it been an accident? Either way, had he enjoyed it?

I looked over to see Adrian, dead white, dead calm. Drilling into me, seeing my every thought.

Adrian

She thinks I hit the deer on purpose? Recharging my batteries? How can she *think* that?

People believe what they see. I can't win.

I ignore that other question, the one clamoring for my attention. Had I enjoyed it? Don't go there. Don't answer that one.

At lunch, Gwen sits alone, and pointedly ignores me.

Conrad asks, "Trouble in paradise?"

"Nah. Another day in Hell."

"Want to come over tonight? Work off some energy?"

"Good idea," I say.

I head over to his house around nine. It's clear and cold, with a wind out of the northwest. A spotlight, mounted on Conrad's house, sends long tree shadows across the ice.

Conrad skates through light and dark, effortlessly, like he was born with blades instead of feet. He gathers himself, then jumps. I don't know what they call it—an axle, maybe—but I'm impressed.

"Hey," I yell. "Nice jump."

He comes to a perfect, controlled stop, sheering slivers of ice off the rink.

"Don't tell anyone you saw that," he says.

"Why not?" I sit down and put on my borrowed skates.

Conrad skates over. "It's embarrassing. My mom made me take figure skating as a kid."

"But you're good."

He laughs. "You're such an expert. C'mon. I'll teach you how to use your stick."

"Uh, Conrad. Figured that one out years ago."

He swings his hockey stick at me and I duck, laughing. I wobble over to where he's set up a line of pucks facing the net. I line up my shot, pull back the stick, whack it a good one. I miss, overbalance, and fall.

"Well done, Bambi," Conrad says, grinning. "Now try that shot again."

This time the puck goes in. I'm lining up for another shot when Conrad says, "So, is it true?"

"Is what true?"

"What Gwen's been telling Joanne," Conrad says.

I whack the puck. It rebounds off the edge of the net. Conrad ducks to avoid getting hit.

"About what?"

Conrad hits a puck smack into the middle of the net. "That you can read Gwen's mind." *Whack.* Another puck hits the net. "That you showed up at a fire and sucked up some woman's soul." *Whack.* "Then you got hungry and killed a deer."

"Do you believe all that?"

"Not really." He skates over, retrieves the pucks and nudges them into a straight line with his hockey stick. "But I have to ask myself, why would Gwen make all that up?"

"She's suspicious. Doesn't trust anyone. Prejudges them.

She's got two sets of rules: one for her and one for the rest of the world. She'll do anything to get what she wants," I say.

"Must be like looking in a mirror," Conrad says.

I've held my anger in all day. Now, it erupts. I launch myself at him, and we land in a snowbank with me on top. He arches and twists, and suddenly I'm facedown in the snow with my arm twisted behind my back.

"Give up?" he asks.

"Never!"

He yanks up on my arm. I grit my teeth.

"Give up?"

"Yeah, whatever." Snow melts down my neck. My teeth chatter.

"Cold?" Conrad asks.

"No."

Conrad sighs, crouches down and helps me get my skates off and my boots on. He holds out his hand, pulls me to my feet. "Friends?"

"I wouldn't want you for an enemy," I say.

He grins, throws a few fake punches my way.

As we walk back up to my car, Conrad asks a question. "Can you read anyone's mind? Or only Gwen's?"

"You really want to know?"

He cranks his neck first one way and then the other. "Not really."

"Good," I say.

"I have nothing to hide, anyway," he says.

"Except being an artist."

"Yeah. There's that."

"I don't get it. What's the big deal?"

He gives me a long look. "Artist guy on the school hockey team?"

"So? Why not?"

"Wrong image." He shrugs.

"So, why'd you show Joanne?" I'm not making polite conversation. I want to know.

"Art is personal, eh? It's like stripping naked. Like baring your soul. Joanne kept saying I didn't open up to her. Didn't show her who I am." He shrugs again. "So I showed her."

"But now everyone knows, right?" I ask. "Your hockey friends and everyone?"

"It was worth the risk," he says. "I was going to lose Joanne. *To you.* So I had to tell her."

"So you owe me one, right?" I say.

"Nah. Don't push your luck."

"You know, you're pretty smart for a dumb jock," I say.

"Yeah. You're okay, too, Bambi."

He bangs the hood of my car in good-bye.

WEDNESDAY, FEBRUARY 5

Gwen

I watched as Melissa approached Adrian at his locker. That figured. Word was that Stone had broken up with her again. Seems she'd slept with another guy. Wow. Big surprise.

She basically threw herself at Adrian. Nuzzled up close, wrapped her arms around him. After a second's hesitation, he returned the embrace.

Like seeks like. I left for the newspaper, knowing how it would end. When I arrived, Doug called me into his office.

"Great job on the fire, kiddo."

"Thanks."

"I've been thinking. I usually hire a student for a summer internship. But you show a lot of promise. Good photos, professional reporting. Would you be interested?"

"I'd love it!" I can barely stay in my chair, I'm so excited.

Doug reached across his desk to shake hands. "You earned it, kiddo. We'll work out the details later, eh?"

Yes!

Adrian

Melissa comes up to my locker after school. A month ago, I would have been all over her. Things change.

"Thank you for defending me the other day." Her eyes well up and drip. She rubs them and smears mascara all over. She looks like a kid trying to be an adult.

"No problem," I say.

Her tears turn to sobs. She presses up against me and puts her arms around me. I read her mind. She needs a hug. It's not so much to ask. I put my arms around her.

Her crying stops after a while. She sniffles, only it comes out loud, like a horse snorting. It takes all my control not to smile.

"Um, look, that night at your house . . . " she says.

I put a finger on her lips. "It'll be our little secret. You won't tell and I won't tell."

"I don't know why I do that," she says. "I'm such a . . . such a—"

"Melissa. Look at me. Don't accept the label, okay? Don't let other people tell you who you are."

She smiles. "You're one of the good guys, Adrian."

"Yeah," I say. "I like to think of myself that way."

THURSDAY, FEBRUARY 6

Gwen

I was eating alone. I took my bookmark out of *Crime and Punishment* and picked up where I had left off.

"Mind if I sit down?"

Melissa? What did she want?

"Free country." I stuffed my face back into the book, pointedly ignoring her.

She sat down beside me. From the corner of my eye, I could see her fiddling with a tissue, ripping it up into tiny pieces.

"I know you saw me with Adrian yesterday—"

"Like I said, free country."

"It wasn't what it looked like. We aren't together or anything. I mean, we went out on a date, but nothing happened."

I kept my eyes on my book, but I was listening.

"And, like, yesterday, I was thanking him—"

"I'll say you were."

"For standing up for me."

I looked up from my book to see tears in Melissa's eyes.

"I had a fight with Stone. Adrian stepped in."

"What a hero," I said.

"Gwen, what happened between you two? I mean, he was bringing you flowers and you guys spent every minute together and then it was suddenly over."

I stared at her. She really thought I'd confide in her?

"I know you don't like me," Melissa went on, "but there's something I need to say."

"I'm not stopping you."

"Back in grade eight, when Stone stood you up for the graduation dance, it wasn't because Joanne paid him."

"I know that."

"I paid him. But not to ask you out."

"I don't get it."

"Stone asked you to the dance on his own. I paid him fifty bucks to *not* go."

"You expect me to believe that? Stone wouldn't have asked me out. I was fat, with braces and glasses. And zits."

"We all had braces and zits," Melissa said with a wry expression. "And no one wore contacts in grade eight."

"But I *was* fat."

"You were also funny and smart. Stone had a thing for you. Still does. Ever notice the way he looks at you?"

"Look, I wouldn't date Stone if he were the last man on the planet."

"That's funny," she said. "He's all I ever wanted."

Her voice was so sad. Had I misjudged her? Did she actually have a heart?

"Anyway, I wanted you to know." Melissa paused, ripped up the tissue into even smaller pieces. "And to say I'm sorry. Better late than never, eh?"

She sniffled, looked at her useless tissue, and then got up.

"Melissa?"

She turned back.

"Thank you."

"You're welcome. Um, I notice you're sitting alone again, now that you broke up with Adrian. . . ."

I was about to say we were never together, but I stopped myself.

"Uh, anyway, like, would you like to sit with us?"

Now was my chance. Put her down, humiliate her, say something scathingly sarcastic. But I remembered what it had been like to be on the receiving end of rejection.

"Okay," I said.

Adrian

I walk into the cafeteria and do a double take. Gwen, sitting with Melissa and her friends? I thought she hated Melissa.

I buy two lunches, one for me, one for Gwen. I deliver hers.

She pretends I'm not there, but she accepts the offering. As I walk away, I hear Melissa ask, "What's with that, anyway?"

"Long story," says Gwen.

I join Conrad and the guys.

"What's going on over there?" Conrad asks.

"No idea. Not a mind reader," I reply.

He grins at me, says nothing.

I tune out the conversation around me and concentrate on reading Gwen's thoughts. She's too busy talking to Melissa to block me.

Melissa is saying to her, "Yeah, anything you want. You only have to go two or three times a week. Want to come with me next time?"

She's talking about kickboxing. Great. As if Gwen isn't lethal enough already.

"So, when are you going to patch it up?" Conrad asks me, looking over at Gwen.

"She won't listen," I said.

"Never figured you for a coward," Conrad says.

"You don't know her."

"You're going to lose her, man."

He's right. She's sitting there, talking to Melissa, laughing, her face animated. She looks incredible—long-sleeved green sweater, jeans, some kind of glossy stuff on her lips. She adjusts her glasses and tucks her hair behind her ears.

"Wish me luck," I say to Conrad.

He gives me a two-thumbs-up gesture. "Go get her, Bambi."

And *that's* supposed to boost my confidence?

My throat goes dry as I walk over. When I get there, I

take a sip of water from Gwen's bottle. I figured I'm entitled. I bought it for her.

"Gwen, could we talk?"

"About what?"

"Can I sit down?"

"No." She likes the way the word feels. She's on top and she knows it.

"Please?"

"Are you begging?"

That's it. I'm leaving. Then I remember why I came.

"Yes. I'm begging you. Want me down on my knees?"

I'd love to see that, she thinks.

So that's what I do. I go down on one knee, right there in the cafeteria. Melissa's mouth drops open. Her friends stare at me.

From across the cafeteria, someone yells, "Yay, Adrian!" Another person shouts, "Whoohoo, Gwen!"

My face is on fire and my knee hurts. The moment stretches on forever.

"Oh, get up already," she says.

I grab onto the edge of the table and pull myself up. Melissa and her friends clap. Three or four other tables join in.

I'm dying, but Gwen is having a great time. Bring Adrian to his knees. Humiliate him in public. But that's okay. If she wants me humble, I'll be humble. Anything she wants.

Gwen

We got our coats and went outside. It was probably the coldest day of the winter.

"Let's sit in my car." He led the way to his red Mustang. The front end was crumpled.

Serves you right, I thought.

By the sudden tightening of his jaw, I saw he caught my thoughts.

He walked around and opened my door first. He was the same old Adrian, playing the role, being chivalrous.

I slid into a contoured bucket seat. The leather felt soft and supple, as if he used leather conditioner. Well, duh. Of course he did.

He turned over the engine and played with the stick shift, running it through the gears. A dark shadow of stubble was the only color on his face. The only sound was the car heater, hissing out warm air. The windshield defrosted before either of us spoke.

"What's that?" he asked, pointing to the blue sky outside. "Snow? There's no clouds."

"Diamond dust," I said. "The moisture in the upper atmosphere freezes as ice crystals. They're fragile. Form only when conditions are just right, often melt before they hit the ground."

He nodded. The silence turned loud.

"Listen," he finally said, "Conrad told me what you told Joanne. About the night of the fire; about the deer. I'd appreciate the chance to explain."

"Go ahead," I said. "No one's stopping you."

Adrian

She's got the upper hand. Again.

My fingers itch for a cigarette. I play with the gearshift,

enjoying the control I have over its movement. It's about the only control I seem to have left.

"The deer was an accident," I tell her. "I didn't see it until it was too late."

"So you finished it off?" she accuses.

"Give me a chance, will you?"

"I'm sorry. Please *do* continue," she says with exaggerated politeness.

Why does she keep pushing me to the edge? I slam my hand on the steering wheel, sounding the horn. She jumps.

"Can't you turn it off? Even for one second?" I say.

"What about the night that woman died in the fire?" she asks, as if I hadn't spoken.

"*That woman* had a name. Celina. But, yeah. It happened again."

"And you can't wait for your next fix," she says.

She sees right through me. She's right. I'm addicted. I love the rush, whether it comes from Celina or a dying deer. Or Gwen.

"This is pointless," I say, yanking my keys out of the ignition.

The motion draws her attention. She stares at my key ring.

At the skull.

Was he there? At the first fire? Is that some kind of souvenir?

"No, it's not like that—" I start to say. Then I see the look in Gwen's eyes. The same look as that night at my house. The same look at the fire. The same as the night I hit the deer.

153

"Get out." My voice shakes.

"What?"

"You heard me. Get out. Before I say something I'll regret."

"Is that another threat?" she sneers.

"Get out!" I'm *this* close to losing it. I reach across her to open the door. A sizzle of energy enters me as my arm brushes against her.

She stomps out, slams the door.

I've had another vision, she sends them to me.

A house. Purple house with yellow shutters. Same house we pass by every day on our way to school. Probably not another house like it in the world.

It's on fire.

Two people stumble out the front door, each carrying a child. But a third child is trapped inside. I see myself, running into the burning house.

I roll down my window. "No way. Find yourself another hero."

I don't need you, she thinks at me.

"What are you going to do?" I yell at her retreating back. "Take photos?"

Without looking back, she gives me the finger.

Another vision hits her.

Camera in her hands, she sneaks up to the sliding glass doors at the back of the house. Through the glass, she takes shot after shot of the arsonist as he pours gasoline around the perimeter of the room and splashes it onto the walls. In the corner farthest from the doors, he places newspapers and rags, soaks them in gas.

Gwen puts down her camera, reaches for her cell phone.

Her attention on dialing, she doesn't see the arsonist cross the room, yank open the door.

He grabs her, drags her inside.

Gwen stops walking. Turns to look back at me.

Midnight. Tomorrow. Don't be late, she sends to me.

"How do you know?" I say.

I checked the weather. It's going to snow tonight. Tomorrow is clear. Moonset is at midnight.

That's how she knows. The moon was setting in her vision. Then I realize something. If she's that sure about the time and place, we can call the police.

"I'm calling the police!" I yell.

I thought of that. It won't work. They'll scare him off. He'll just strike later.

"They'll put the house under surveillance, Gwen. He won't have a chance to strike."

Will they keep the house under surveillance forever, Adrian? For years? Sooner or later, he'll burn it down. What must happen will happen.

"I'm not going!" I shout.

Only, we both know I will.

FRIDAY, FEBRUARY 7

Adrian

I leave an hour early. Here's my plan. Be there when the arsonist arrives. Use *the voice* to subdue him. Make an anonymous call to the police. Go home.

I won't get hurt and Gwen won't get her story. Works for me.

I park a few hundred yards down the highway, on the shoulder. I should be able to see the arsonist drive by. He'll park in the lane, fifty feet from the house. Gwen's vision showed that.

I open my thermos and pour some coffee. I light up a cigarette and wait. A moment later, I butt it out frantically. A car is coming. I hunch down in the seat, hoping he didn't see the glow of my cigarette.

I touch his mind. I'm safe.

My boots squeak in the snow as I walk down the highway. I hope he can't hear me. I tap into his thoughts.

The last one on my list. Foster parents. They pretend to care, but the first thing you do wrong and whammo *you're out of there. Payback time!*

So that's his motive. Revenge. Sick reasoning. If I can't have a home, why should they? But I guess you have to be sick to torch a house, especially if there might be people inside.

The lane leading to the house is lined with evergreens. I slip between the shadows, welcoming their protection. I pass the guy's car and memorize the license plate.

As I get closer, I see him. He walks around to the back of the house, checking windows as he goes. He's carrying a gas can and a shopping bag. I see newspapers and a few chunks of wood sticking up from it. Kindling. He reaches the back door, puts his hand on the handle.

I step out of the darkness into a pale wash of moonlight.

"Back off from that door," I order, using *the voice.*

He whirls around, startled, to face me.

"What the—?"

"Put down the gasoline," I say.

He gives a half-laugh. "Hey, man, can you believe it? Locked out of my own house. Stupid, eh?"

"You can't lie to me," I say, walking toward him. "Back off."

157

"You aren't a part of this," he says, not laughing this time. "Go away and forget what you saw, okay?"

"How many others?" I demand.

He wavers, then says, "Two here. Two last winter, up in Blue Lake. I'm done now. So don't complicate things."

I'm surprised he tells me that. But I remember what Gwen wrote in her article about arson. When caught, the arsonist usually confesses readily. He may even be proud of his track record.

I put all the authority of The Power into my voice. "I'm ordering you to stand down. *Now.*"

"Whatever you say, man." He walks toward me, sets down the gasoline, sets down the bag.

I grab my phone and start to dial the police. *The voice never fails.*

But then I catch his thoughts. He's grabbing a piece of wood from the bag.

And I am too slow to stop him.

Gwen

All day, the visions shifted around me in a kaleidoscope of possibilities. What was real? I couldn't tell.

I planned to leave at eleven thirty, to give myself time to meet Adrian at midnight. But at eleven, a vision hit me with hurricane force.

> *Adrian confronts a man who is carrying a gas can and a bag of kindling. He uses his voice of command, but it doesn't work. The arsonist swings a piece of*

wood at Adrian, catching him in the head.
Adrian drops to the snow. He's not moving.

My Mom was in bed. I wondered if I should leave a note. No, I decided. With a bit of luck, she'd never know I was gone.

I found Adrian's car parked on the highway. How long had he been here? Five minutes? An hour? The moon was setting, throwing dark shadows between the trees.

I ran up the middle of the lane, not worried about meeting the arsonist. If my vision was correct, he was already gone. I reached the house. Black smoke billowed out of the upper story. Red flames shot out of a window.

By the fiery glow, I saw Adrian push himself to a sitting position.

"Are you okay?" I asked, dropping to my knees beside him. I took a closer look at him. No blood, not that I could see.

"Yeah," he said, rubbing the side of his head. "I'll live."

Two people, a man and a woman, burst out of the back door of the house, each carrying a child. They sank to the snowy ground, coughing.

"There's one left," said Adrian, standing up. He wavered, as if he hadn't quite got his balance back.

He ran into the house.

Adrian

I must be crazy. I'm running into a burning building. I have no idea why.

Yeah, I do. To prove to Gwen I'm one of the good guys.

159

My head pounds with every step. I'm dizzy from the blow to my head. Heat and smoke batter me, nearly force me back. The family room is engulfed in flame—the couch, the bookcase, the walls.

Gwen's mental voice reaches me. *Stairs on the left. Bedrooms upstairs.*

I rush up the stairs. Flames lick up the wall. The carpet smolders beneath my boots.

I crawl along the hallway, staying low. I can feel a child in the second bedroom. I find her huddled on the floor, grab her, head for the stairs.

No! Gwen sees me carrying a child, the stairs collapsing and a wall falling on top of us. *The window. Go out the window.*

The window? I can't see any window. The smoke is too thick. I crawl along the floor, coughing, choking. I find a wall. Reach up. Find the window. I push it open, burning my hands. The fire roars toward me, flaming out into the night. I fumble with the screen, find the release, and send it toppling to the ground below.

The child clings to my neck in a stranglehold. I loosen her grip, and drop her through the open window. Gwen is waiting below.

Gwen catches her, gets knocked over, rolls in the snow. But she's okay. They're both okay.

I climb out backwards, hang for a second, and let go.

It gets a bit confused after that. My hands hurt. My lungs hurt. I hear sirens.

"Let's go," I say to Gwen.

"You go. Get to the hospital. You could have a concussion," she says. "I'm staying. There's a story here."

"And how will you explain to the police that you just *happened* to be here?" I ask.

"I'll make something up," she says.

"Go home, Gwen. You've done enough damage for one night."

I feel the hurt in her mind, but I'm past caring. I'm sick of being her puppet.

The parents reach us. The father takes the child from Gwen's arms. He coughs to clear his lungs, says, "Thank you. Who are you?"

"No one was here," I say, using *the voice*.

"But," Gwen says.

"No buts. No heroes. No story," I say.

She glares at me as if she wants to hurl an energy ball at me. "Okay, fine, have it your way," she huffs at me.

"It's about time," I mutter.

I turn to the couple and use *the voice*. This time I feel Gwen's energy join mine, magnifying my power.

"You saved all your children," I say, slowly and distinctly. "You and your wife. She's a brave woman."

"A brave woman, my wife," says the man, with considerable feeling.

"Hope you're happy," Gwen says, as we walk back to our cars.

"Ecstatic," I assure her.

SATURDAY, FEBRUARY 8

Gwen

Last night, I had a dream.

> *Adrian loads the trunk of his car with boxes, throws a duffle bag into the backseat. I stand in the driveway, watching.*
>
> *A glowing silver cord connects us. The Power flows through it, from him to me and back to him. His aura flames blue.*
>
> *He gets into the car, drives away. The cord*

stretches, growing faint, turns pencil thin. Finally, it breaks.

I awoke, soaked in cold, slippery sweat.

I borrowed Mom's car to drive over at around noon. He met me at the front door.

I almost didn't recognize him. Under his dark-rimmed glasses, his eyes were light gray, the color of the sky just before sunrise. They were cool, but not as mesmerizing as his unnaturally blue contacts.

"That was the whole point," he said, clearly reading my mind. He stood squarely in the doorway, dressed in a dark blue T-shirt and jeans. The palms of his hands were wrapped in gauze, leaving his fingertips exposed. I felt a stab of guilt at that.

"May I come in?"

He shrugged, turned, and went down the stairs.

"I guess that's a *yes*," I said, under my breath.

"Where are your parents?" I called down to him, as I removed my hat and gloves.

"Gone."

"When are they coming back?" Got out of my coat, hung it on the hook on the wall.

"Later."

"Did you tell them about last night?" Took off my boots.

"No. They left before I came out of my room."

"Are you going to tell them?" Walked downstairs.

"Don't know."

I reached his room. An open suitcase sat on his bed.

"What are you doing?" I asked, watching him take a pile of jeans from his wardrobe and place them in the suitcase.

"Should be obvious," he replied.

"Where?"

"To live with my brother in Milwaukee. I figure fifteen hours away might just be far enough."

"Can we talk?" I asked.

"Isn't that what we're doing?" He placed several T-shirts on top of the jeans.

"Please?" I moved the suitcase. "Sit down?"

"You're begging?"

"Yes." I said, patting the bed.

"I'm more comfortable over here," he said, sitting down in the chair at his computer desk. He started to fold his arms, grimaced, rested his bandaged hands awkwardly on his knees.

"You should see a doctor," I said.

"Already did."

"What'd he say?"

"Superficial burns. Nothing to concern yourself over."

I'd never seen him so angry before. He held it in, but it showed in the tension in his jaw, the flatness of his voice.

"That surprises you?" he asks. "That I'm angry? Just because you've knocked me to the ground with a fireball. Made me beg. Made me risk my life, over and over—running toward a train wreck, crawling over unsafe ice, going into a burning house."

"Whoa. Wait. You did those things yourself," I said, my own temper flaring.

"Why, Gwen?" He stood up, crossed the room, grabbed a pack of cigarettes. He shook one out and fumbled, trying to light a match.

"Want me to light that?" I asked.

"Don't do me any favors." He threw the cigarettes across the room. They hit the wall and slid down. "I'm quitting, anyway.

"Tell me," he continued, in a belligerent tone, "why did I risk my life last night?"

"You tell me," I retorted.

He swore and swung around as if he was going to punch the wall behind him. At the last second, he stopped. I don't know if it was self-control or if he couldn't make a fist.

He laughed shakily. "I wish you could read my mind, Gwen, like I read yours. It hurts to make a fist."

"Let me see," I said, getting up and reaching toward him.

His reaction was so violent it startled me. "Don't touch me."

"What is *wrong* with you?"

Another half-laugh. "You were right about me. I *am* addicted. But not just to The Power. To you."

To me? You're just saying that. To get The Power. That's all you ever wanted.

He smacked his hand down on his desk, then swore violently. "When will you trust me? What do I have to do?"

"Stop lying," I shouted back. "Stop manipulating me. Stop using me."

He stood up, paced back and forth. "Look in a mirror, Gwen. You used me to get your newspaper stories. You let me do your dirty work. And you sat back, nice and safe, taking your pictures and writing up your stories. You didn't even try to help."

"The universe is set in its course. You can't change what—"

"You don't try! You have all this power, these dreams, these visions—and you sit back and do nothing. Did you try to pin down the time and location of the last fire? Notify the police?" He's shouting now, waving his arms. "That would have ruined your story, wouldn't it? A fire, a death. It all makes such a *good* story."

I couldn't believe he was saying this. It was so unfair. I felt the rage building, and—

Adrian

I'm not ready for it. The fireball she hurls at me. It catches me by surprise.

"Do you have any idea how that feels? Are you trying to stop my heart?" I gasp.

She glares at me. *You deserved it.*

"Why? Because I dared question your motives?"

This time she really whacks me. It's like a physical blow, right in the gut. My heart beats out of control and my head nearly explodes. And then, I laugh. It's a wheezy little laugh, but it still feels good.

"You're as addicted as I am," I choke out.

"What?"

I suck in air. "How did it feel, Gwen? Want to zap me again? You can't wait for your next fix, can you?"

This time it's a ton of bricks falling on me. I'm writhing,

and opening my mouth, but no sounds come out. Gwen panics. She thinks I'm dying. I'm thinking she might be right. Eventually, the pain eases and I can breathe again.

"I'm sorry," I risk saying.

"Me, too," she says.

"Conrad says we're alike."

"Do you think so?" Gwen asks.

She snorts. I laugh. We both relax a bit.

"You know, Conrad's pretty smart," I say.

"Uh, huh?"

"Yeah. He told me some things. About his art. That he didn't tell anyone at first, because it didn't fit the hockey-player image. But he showed Joanne, because his art showed who he was. He said it was like baring your soul."

She's listening.

"He also said I should do that with you."

"Bare your soul?"

"Pretty much," I say. "You won't hit a man when he's down, will you?"

This is a new side of him, she's thinking. *I like it.*

I'm thinking that won't last long.

"Let's go sit in front of the fire." Closer to the stairs, I think. Not as far to go when you walk out on me, again.

We move into the family room. The fire is low, so I open the glass door of the woodstove and grab a log with my fingertips. I toss it in awkwardly, and it lands with a thump. The heat from the fire reaches the palms of my hands. It feels like I'm scorching them all over again. I bite my lip, hold it in.

Gwen doesn't notice. She's over by the sliding glass

door, looking out at the white of the frozen lake and the perfect blue of a cloudless sky. Ice crystals shimmer in the air. Diamond dust.

She sinks down on the couch, waits for me to speak. I sit a few feet away, and stare into the fire, wondering how to begin. I catch myself tapping my fingers on my leg.

He does that when he's nervous, she thinks.

That makes me smile. I can't hide from her. I might as well get this over with.

"You were right about me, at first," I say. "I did those things, brought you flowers, flattered you and—"

I knew it. He only wanted The Power. Not me.

"Yes," I say. "At first. But then, you changed and—"

Cutting my hair. Dying it. Green contacts.

"I wasn't a fan of the red hair," I say. "Or the green eyes. You looked like a Melissa clone."

"But you said you liked it."

"It's what you wanted to hear."

"And when you said I wasn't fat?"

I hesitate.

"I'd appreciate some honesty, for once," she says.

I chose my words carefully. "I think *you'd* be happier with the way you look if you lost ten or fifteen pounds. The kickboxing will help. And no more lettuce-and-water diets. Your body was in starvation mode."

A wave of hurt hits me. "But," I go on, "if you want to change, do it for *you*. Not me. I like you the way you are."

"You're saying that because it's what I want to hear," she says.

"No. I'm saying that because you asked me to be honest,"

I say. "Besides, if you lose weight, your boobs will shrink."

She gasps, then laughs, and lightly swats my arm. That sends a sharp pain through my hands. I hide my reaction.

"Hey, you asked for honesty," I protest. "The truth is that you look like a sexy eyeglasses model—smart, and a little intimidating."

I bask for a moment in the warmth of her smile.

"What did you mean before?" she asks. "You said you weren't just addicted to The Power. You were addicted to me. Was that one of your lines?"

"No. I admit, at first, I wanted to be near you because of The Power. The rush was better than anything. Better than sex."

Wouldn't know, she thinks.

"Trust me. It is. Something happens when we are together—"

"Synergy," she interrupts. "Two forces, working together to produce a greater effect than the sum of their parts."

"If you say so. Anyway, that's how it started. But later, after the night you came here, I wanted *you*. At first, it was because I couldn't have you."

"And you aren't used to rejection?" she asks, wryly.

"No. I'm not," I say, honestly. "And I'm not used to someone beating me at my own game."

"I don't play games."

I laugh out loud. "Oh, yes, you do. The hunger strike was the best. I respected you for that. And manipulating me, getting me to do the hero thing for you. That was a good one, too."

Her emotions turn defensive *Deserved it for—*

"Shhh." I put a finger on her lips. "Still my turn."

The touch sends a surge of energy through her, back to me, back to her, like an alternating current. I enjoy that for a moment, because now I have to do the hard part.

"I need to say some things, and I'm pretty sure you'll hate me when I'm finished," I say. "All I ask is that you hear me out."

She nods, and I take a deep breath. I've heard confession is good for the soul. I've heard wrong. Confession is like pulling your entrails out with a meat hook.

"I lied to you. I told you I could only read *your* thoughts," I say.

"You mean you—?"

"Since the day I gave you the plant. You opened a door in my mind. I could hear everyone."

"What? Everyone? Joanne, too?'

"Everyone."

"I can't believe you! That's the ultimate invasion of privacy. You just waltzed in, without permission, and saw what they were thinking?"

"Pretty much."

I feel the energy build in her and I flinch, then brace myself. This one's going to hurt.

Miraculously, she reins in her anger. "Go on," she says.

I take a deep breath. "The night I hit the deer. I didn't hit it on purpose, I swear. But, you were right. I fed off it. The same thing happened the night Celina died."

My voice goes rough and I cough to clear my throat.

"Both times you saw through me. Saw how much I craved The Power. I couldn't hide from you. That look you gave me. It nearly killed me."

"I'm sor—"

"No. Don't be sorry." I clear my throat again. "There's more. That night that I invited you over and wouldn't let you leave? I pinned you down on the couch and—"

"You didn't—" she starts to interrupt.

"Uh, Gwen, I'm pretty sure I only have the courage to say this once."

"Go on."

I get up, pace in front of the fire.

"If I had walked in on that, if I had seen some guy holding you down like that, shouting at you, I'd have pounded the living—" I glance at her. She gets it. "The worst thing is that I *enjoyed* it. I *liked* having the upper hand. I *liked* being in control."

I risk looking at her. She has tears in her eyes. I look down at my hands and continue.

"And then I caught your emotions. Hurt. Fear. I went into your mind. I saw myself through your eyes. I didn't like what I saw.

"When you left, I tried to justify it. Tried to deny it. Wouldn't let myself think about it."

"I attacked you first," she says.

"You attacked me because I grabbed you and wouldn't let you go."

"Nothing happened," Gwen says.

I get up, and throw another log on the fire, glad of the pain it causes me.

"We both know that's not true," I say. "It scares me to realize how little control I had that night. It was as if The Power had taken over."

It takes her a long time to speak. "The hyacinth bloomed," she says. *For forgiveness.* She moves closer, so our legs are touching. "I feel like I'm seeing you for the first time."

"You are."

"Why didn't you let me in sooner?" she asks.

"Let *you* in? I barely let myself in," I say.

She smiles. "Are you still going to leave?"

"What do the visions tell you?"

"Could go either way."

"You choose."

"Stay," she says.

"I'm afraid. What if The Power takes over? What if I use it against you?"

"And make me do something I don't want to do?" she asks. "You can't. I have my own power."

"C'mon, Gwen. I can command you with a word."

"Prove it."

"No. I'm not using *the voice* on you."

"Afraid of losing?" she asks.

"Afraid of winning. Of knowing I can control you."

"You won't win." She's serious. She thinks she can take me.

"Fine," I say, getting to my feet. "Don't say I didn't warn you."

I draw on The Power. I use *the voice.* "Come to me, Gwen. Kiss me."

Gwen

He drew The Power around himself like a cloak. He pitched his voice hypnotically low, and mesmerized me with his gaze. I stood close, almost touching. I heard his breathing, shallow, fast. Inhaled the spiciness of his cologne. Felt the heat from his body. Standing on my toes, I reached up to kiss him. He kissed back, his lips hard and mean.

"I rest my case," he said, slumping back into the chair by his desk.

"You dim-witted, idiotic, useless excuse for a person," I retorted. "I *wanted* to kiss you. And for your information, that was a lousy kiss."

"You only *think* you wanted to because I planted the suggestion in your mind," he said.

"Fine. Do it again. Make me do something else."

His eyes narrowed. "Gwen, take off your clothes for me."

"No."

He drew The Power to him once again. Said slowly, softly, "Take off your clothes, Gwen."

"No."

"Take. Them. Off."

Very slowly, I pulled my sweater up, baring my midriff. Half an inch, an inch . . . then I stopped. I yanked the sweater back down. "No, thanks," I said. "I really don't feel like it right now."

He laughed, but it came out more like a bark. He took off his glasses, awkward because of the bandages, and wiped his eyes with the back of one hand. "That's a relief."

"What? You don't want to see me with my clothes off?" I teased.

He gulped. "Oh, no, I don't mean that. I mean, of course I do. I mean—" He laughed. "You're right. I can't win with you, can I?"

I gave him a smug smile. "Nope. You aren't even in my league."

He looked at me thoughtfully. "There's one thing I don't understand. Why didn't *the voice* work on the arsonist last night?"

"You need me," I said, suddenly realizing it was true. "You can't do it on your own. It has to be the two of us, working together."

"No, way. I've done it without you. Made some guy sell me cigarettes without checking my ID. And this girl. Mandy. Got her to knock fifty percent off the price of my new coat."

"Adrian, would you mind putting the kettle on? I'd like a cup of tea," I asked sweetly.

"What? Right now?" He glanced at his bandaged hands.

"Yes. I'd love a cup of tea right now."

Grumbling, he stomped up the stairs.

"Adrian?" I called. "I changed my mind."

He trudged back down. "What are you doing? Playing me?"

"Making a point," I said. "Sometimes persuasion is just that. Simple persuasion."

"Oh," he said, sitting down beside me. "You could be right. But wait a minute. Mr. Fogerty. Remember? You were there. I ordered him not to drive out onto the ice. He ignored me."

My throat constricted. He'd been honest with me. I owed him the same back.

"I think we have to work together," I said. "I think we have to want the same thing."

"Sure. We wanted to stop him," Adrian said. He drew in a sharp breath as he read my mind. "Unless—"

"I very much wanted that story," I said in a whisper.

I searched his face, waiting for him to condemn me, like I had condemned him so many times.

"Thank you for letting *me* in," he said, brushing his bandaged hand against mine.

"You should be the one hating me," I said. "I risked your life so many times."

He smiled. "There was some truth in what you said, Gwen. I did like the glory."

"Too bad it wasn't worth it," I said.

"What do you mean?"

"We saved Mr. Dean from a train wreck, but he died in a car accident."

"I didn't know that." Adrian frowned.

"And Mr. Fogerty. After you rescued him from drowning, he had a heart attack and slipped into a coma. Died a few days ago."

"He did?"

"Yeah, don't you read the paper?"

"Only if I'm in it," he said, with a sheepish grin. "What about the little boy, the one who was locked out of his house."

"I followed up on that. He's fine. So's the drunk."

"What drunk?"

"This guy in an alley. He was passed-out drunk so Joanne and I called the police."

"Wait," said Adrian, "did he have lice?"

"I think so. Why?"

"I heard you say, 'Can lice jump?' I was buying my coat at the time."

"We were already linked," I said.

"Wait a minute. What were you doing that first day of school? You left for the newspaper."

"Taking a picture of the house that burned down."

"What kind of picture?" he asked.

"There was a poster, a skull. Oh, your key ring."

"Yeah. My key ring," he said. "I was already reading your mind."

"I'm sorry. I misjudged you."

"Prejudged me, you mean," he said. "Thought you knew everything about me. Thanks for calling me a jerk, by the way."

"Hey. That's not fair. You were mucking around in my mind."

"Yeah, like you don't muck in mine."

"What do you mean? I can't read your mind."

"Read it, no. Control it, yes. I can't block the visions you send me. Can't block your emotions. Can't block your pain or hunger or fear. And do me a favor, okay? Take something for your period next time."

"Hey!" I pulled a tiny portion of The Power to me, a scratchy ball of energy, and held it in my hand.

"Go ahead," he said, jutting out his chin. "Bully!"

I grinned, but tossed the crackling, spitting ball of energy harmlessly aside.

"So, why does it only work part of the time?" I asked, getting back to what we'd been talking about. "Why did Dean and Fogerty die after we saved them, but the little boy and the old drunk live?"

For some reason, the color drained out of Adrian's face. "How about I make you that tea now?"

He jumped up and started back up the steps.

My stomach twisted. "Tea? Why? What are you hiding?"

"Nothing."

"You're lying. I can read you like a book."

"You won't like it," he said, sitting back down.

"I'm a big girl," I said.

"Patterns," he said. "Don't you see the pattern?"

Adrian

I wish I couldn't, but I feel her reaction. Heart speeding up, mouth going dry.

"Go on," she says.

"Mr. Dean made the front page, right? He died. Then we saved Mr. Fogerty. You printed it in the paper. Dramatic rescue. Only, he's dead, too. You published Celina's story, pictures and all. She died in the fire."

"So?" she croaks.

"The little boy is okay. You didn't print his story. Didn't develop the photos. Remember? I erased your pictures. Did you print a story about the drunk?"

"No. Joanne wouldn't let me."

"So, they only die when you print the story in the paper," I say.

Her mind refuses to go there. Refuses to confront the truth.

"But, wait. What about that woman. Celina? She died before the story appeared in the paper. We couldn't save her."

I choose my next words carefully and say them as gently as possible. "Gwen, how hard did you try to save her?"

"I don't know what you mean."

Yes, she does, but she doesn't want to face it.

"I repeat, how hard did you try to save her? To pull the vision in closer, to figure out the time and location, maybe contact the police?"

She looks at me in alarm.

"You went to that fire to get a story," I say. "Not to save a life."

She gets a sharp pain in her stomach. "I think I'm going to be sick."

She's not kidding. I rush her to the bathroom and she sinks to the floor beside the toilet. I run the cold water, soak some washcloths, put them on her neck and forehead.

"Take deep breaths," I say.

"Why are you being so nice?" she gasps.

"I hate throwing up," I say.

"Oh."

"Yeah, oh. Feeling better yet?"

"You should know," she says with the shadow of a smile.

"Yeah. C'mon. I'll bring you a soda. Help settle your stomach."

She lets me lead her to the couch.

I dash upstairs. I grab diet ginger ale, add ice, then rush back down.

She's crying the way a small child cries: out loud, sobbing, gasping for air. I try to put my arm around her, but she flinches and pulls away.

"How can you even look at me?" she says.

"We all make mistakes."

"Yours don't kill people," she says. "It all makes sense. Checks and balances. We do a good deed, but if we benefit, the good deed is erased."

"We didn't know. We'll do better next time," I tell her.

"Oh, Adrian," she says, starting a fresh flood of tears. "Last night. If I'd printed their story—"

"Shhh," I tell her. "You didn't."

"Only because you stopped me."

I want to hold her, but my hands hurt too much. I grab a box of tissues from the bathroom and hand them to her. She yanks out four or five, dries her eyes, blows her nose.

"My mother had the dreams, too. She saved a child, but the child later died. She figured it was preordained. But, it's because she received a medal from the town. For bravery. The dreams don't bring death. We do, my mother and me."

"That's not true."

"The worst thing is," she goes on, "I can't even tell her. I think she'd have a nervous breakdown."

"You can tell me," I say.

She sniffles, blows her nose again. "I thought you were

dangerous. Someone who would stop at nothing to get what he wanted. I was so wrong about you."

I tuck a stray piece of hair behind her ear. "You were entirely right about me. But thanks for the vote of confidence."

"I was just as bad. Even worse. Socking you with energy balls. That first time, it was purely instinctive. But you're right. It's addictive. It makes me feel so strong, so powerful. Like today. I *wanted* to hurt you. And, I *did* I hurt you, didn't I?"

"No, not so much," I say.

"Liar. You asked if I was trying to stop your heart. Everything I accused you of doing, I did. Only worse."

"Shhh."

"You have to leave," she says, abruptly.

"I'm staying," I tell her. "We've been given a gift. That's why my father brought me here. We're meant to work together."

"We're doing a lousy job so far," she says, with a trace of her old sarcasm.

"We'll do better," I say. "Drink your soda."

"Okay," she says.

"That's what I like," I joke. "A girl who does what she's told."

Gwen snorts, gets soda up her nose, coughs. "Yeah, right. Like that's going to happen."

A log crackles in the woodstove, releasing pine scent into the air. The flames leap, red and gold, like Gwen's eyes when they glow with The Power.

"You were so beautiful," I say. "The last time you were here."

She gets the image in her mind of us in my bedroom, standing in front of my mirror.

"Not that," I say. "Uh, though you were beautiful then, too. I meant when you knocked me down with those fireballs of yours. You were bathed in white light, like some kind of avenging spirit. You were so strong. So formidable. I liked that. But I didn't admit it. Not even to myself."

"Why?"

"Because of the power it gives you over me," I say.

"Oh."

"Yeah, oh," I say. "Look, I don't usually ask permission to kiss a girl, but considering our history, I think it might be a wise move."

"You've got to be kidding." *My face all blotchy, my eyes all puffy.*

"Will you let me kiss you?" I ask.

"Yes."

The couch is only two steps away. It feels like miles.

I sit beside her. She turns to me, but she's thinking, *I don't know how to do this.*

"Trust me," I say, leaning in close.

The Power rushes through her, through me.

"No," I say. "No Power."

I'm not sure if she turns it off or if I do. But when I kiss her, there's no rush of Power. There's just her lips, soft and sweet.

I like that, she thinks. *Like it very much.*

I start to put my arm around her, but as I do, my hand hits the couch. I try to suppress my cry of pain, but I can't.

She gives me a suspicious look. "Let me see."

"No. It's okay."

"Now!" she orders.

"Yes, ma'am," I say.

I wince as she unwraps the gauze on my right hand.

She gasps. "You said they were superficial."

"I lied."

I grit my teeth as she unwraps my left hand. It's the bad one. Deep red, blistered.

"I'm so sorry," she says.

"Don't be. It looks bad, but it's only second degree. Mild second degree. Shouldn't even scar. I'll be good as new in a few weeks."

"Did the doctor even treat you? Give you anything?" She's worried about me. I savor the newness and sweetness of that.

"Yes, the doctor treated me. Told me to stay hydrated, gave me a tetanus booster, antibiotics, and painkillers."

"Are you taking the painkillers?"

"What do you think?"

She thinks I'm not taking them. She's right. I hate being fuzzy-headed.

"I had a dream last night," she says.

"I know."

"About you going away."

"Yes."

"If you did that, we'd lose The Power."

"Yes."

"But you were packing."

"If I can't have you, I don't want The Power." I know she's thinking about that night. *If you had to give up The Power to have me, would you?*

"What if you can have both?" Gwen asks me.

"I'll take both."

She looks at me for a long time, then puts her arms around my neck. She doesn't know much about kissing, but she's a quick learner. When we finally break apart, we're both a bit breathless.

"So, where do we go from here?" she asks.

"We could set a few rules. No manipulation, for one, I'd say."

"No games," she says.

"I'd appreciate no more fireballs."

"No hiding," she says. "Total, brutal honesty."

"That's it! The price!"

"What price?"

"My mother said every gift carries a price. This is it. No hiding. Not from ourselves. Not from each other."

"Big price."

"Big gift."

"It won't be easy," I warn. "We'll argue every step of the way. We'll fight. We'll slip back into old habits."

"I'm willing to risk that," she says.

"You're on."

She smiles. "Bet you can't kiss me before I throw a little sizzler at you."

I smile back.

I love a good challenge, eh?

About the Author

DEBORAH LYNN JACOBS says, "The most challenging aspect of writing this book was exploring how The Power changed both Gwen and Adrian. Some scenes, where they came to terms with the darkness inside of them, were hard to write. But to back away from the deeper issues wouldn't have been telling the complete story.

"I attempted to explore all aspects of power, including the concept of psychic powers. It was a fascinating journey for me, and I'd like to invite you along. Just warning you, though. These aren't nice people. They'll stop at nothing to get what they want!"

Deborah Lynn Jacobs lived in Canada, where the book is set, most of her life. She presently resides in Wisconsin with her husband. Her two children have left for college, probably to avoid the question, "Would you mind taking a look at this?" This is Debbie's first novel for older teens.